Oh, dear God. If Alexandra hadn't been sitting down, she would have fallen. Jordan had always been able to make her knees weak with that beautiful, clever mouth. Pictures bloomed in her head: she could see herself sweeping everything off his desk. Pushing him across it...

She was practically hyperventilating now.

'Jordan. This is a bad idea.' She did her best to drag her common sense from where it was hiding. 'I... This wasn't meant to be a seduction.'

'No. But it could be.' He moistened her lower lip with the tip of his tongue, making her wish it was her skin he was moistening.

'Alex...' His voice was low and sexy.

Oh, God. She was seconds away from losing her self-control. From losing her mind. But his fingers were caressing her wrist, feeling the pulse thudding here.

She tried again. 'I was just being nice. Doing what I'd do for any colleague.'

Liar. He didn't actually say it, but then again he didn't need to. They both knew.

Kate Hardy lives in Norwich, in the east of England, with her husband, two young children, one bouncy spaniel, and too many books to count! When she's not busy writing romance or researching local history, she helps out at her children's schools. She also loves cooking—spot the recipes sneaked into her books! (They're also on her website, along with extracts and stories behind the books.) Writing for Mills & Boon® has been a dream come true for Kate—something she wanted to do ever since she was twelve. She says it's the best of both worlds, because she gets to learn lots of new things when she's researching the background to a book: add a touch of passion, drama and danger, a new gorgeous hero every time, and it's the perfect job!

Kate's always delighted to hear from readers, so do drop in to her website at www.katehardy.com

A recent title by the same author:

A MOMENT ON THE LIPS

Kate also writes for Mills & Boon® Medical™ Romances. Her titles include:

ITALIAN DOCTOR, NO STRINGS ATTACHED
ST PIRAN'S: THE FIREMAN AND NURSE LOVEDAY
  (St Piran's Hospital)

THE EX
WHO HIRED HER

BY
KATE HARDY

First published in Great Britain 2012
by Mills & Boon, an imprint of Harlequin (UK) Limited.
Harlequin (UK) Limited, Eton House, 18-24 Paradise Road,
Richmond, Surrey TW9 1SR

© Pamela Brooks 2

ISBN: 978 0 263 2

Harlequin (UK) polic
and recyclable produ
forests. The logging a.. .... process conform to the
legal environmental regulations of the country of origin.

Printed and bound in Great Britain
by CPI Antony Rowe, Chippenham, Wiltshire

THE EX
WHO HIRED HER

For Lizzie Lamb and Jasper, with love.

CHAPTER ONE

XANDRA BENNETT.

Jordan would just bet she'd changed the spelling of her name, on the grounds that it made her sound more like a marketing hotshot than plain 'Sandra'. He just hoped there was enough substance to back up the style. Maybe there would be; the recruitment agency had obviously thought enough of her to ask Field's for a last-minute interview. Though, after an entire day listening to the bright and not-so-bright ideas of the people who were desperate to become the next marketing manager of Field's department store, Jordan wasn't really in the mood for someone who was all style and glitz.

Last one, he told himself. Last one, and then I can get on with my work.

His PA opened the door. 'Ms Bennett.'

And, as Xandra Bennett walked into his office, Jordan forgot how to breathe.

It was her.

Of all the department stores in all the towns in all the world, she walked into his.

Different name, different hair, and she'd clearly swapped her glasses for contact lenses, but it was definitely her. Alexandra Porter. His whole body tingled. Last time he'd seen her, she'd been eighteen, with mousy-brown hair that fell almost to her waist when he'd loosened it from its customary plait. And she'd worn clothing typical of a shy eighteen-year-old girl: scruffy trainers, nondescript jeans and baggy T-shirts that hid her curves.

Now, she looked every inch the marketing professional. A sharp, well-cut business suit that flattered her curves without making them look ostentatious; a sleek jaw-length bob with highlights so skilfully done that the copper and gold strands looked as though they'd been brought out naturally by the sun; and high-end designer heels that made her legs look as if they went on for ever.

And she still had a mouth that sent shivers through him.

He pushed the thought away. He didn't want to think about Alexandra Porter and her lush, generous mouth. The mouth he'd once taught how to kiss.

She masked it quickly, but he'd been watching her closely enough to see the shock on her face. She recognised him, too, and hadn't expected to see him here, either…or had she? He didn't trust her as far as he could drop his pen onto the desk. Back then she'd turned out to be a manipulative liar, and that wasn't the kind of personality trait that changed with age. Was Bennett the man she'd dumped him for? Or had she then dumped *him* as soon as she'd found someone else who could offer her more?

Maybe he should tell her that the position was already filled and he wasn't going to do any more interviews. Except that would mean explaining his reasons to his co-interviewers—explanations he'd rather not have to give.

Jordan Smith.

Alexandra felt sick to her stomach. He was the last person she'd expected to see. Ten years ago, she'd vowed never to have anything to do with him again. She'd never forgiven him for not being there when she'd needed him most. For lying to her. For letting her down. It had taken her years to rebuild her life; and now, just when her dreams were in reach, he was right in her way all over again.

The tall, slightly gangly student she'd known had filled out; he was far from being fat, but his shoulders were broader and his build more muscular. His mouth still had that sensual curve, promising pleasure—not that she wanted to remember how much pleasure his mouth was capable of giving.

The scruffy jeans and T-shirt he'd usually worn back then had been replaced by a designer suit and what looked like a handmade shirt and a silk tie. There was the faintest touch of silver at his temples—well, of course hair that dark would show the grey quickly. And he definitely had an air of authority. He'd grown into his looks; more than that, he'd grown into the kind of man who just had to breathe to have women falling at his feet.

As the CEO of Field's, Jordan Smith would have the final say over who got the job.

Which left her...where? On the reject pile, because she'd be a permanent reminder of his guilt—of the fact that he'd abandoned her when she was eighteen and pregnant with his baby? Or would he give her the job, even if she wasn't the best candidate, because he felt he owed it to her for wrecking her life all those years ago? And, if he did offer her the job, would she take it, knowing that she'd have to work with him?

The questions whizzed round her head. Then she realised that one of the panel had said something to her and was waiting for a reply. Oh, great. Now they'd think she had the attention span of a gnat and would be a complete liability rather than an asset to the firm. Bye, bye, new job. Well, she had nothing to lose now. She might as well treat this as a practice interview. Afterwards, instead of licking her wounds, she could analyse her performance and see where she needed to sharpen up, ready for the next interview.

'I'm so sorry. I'm afraid I didn't catch that,' she said, giving the older man an apologetic smile.

'I'm Harry Blake, the personnel manager,' he said, smiling back. 'This is Gina Davidson, the deputy store manager.' He paused for long enough to let Alexandra exchange a greeting and shake the deputy manager's hand. 'And this is Jordan Smith, the CEO.'

Jordan had to be a good twenty years younger than his colleagues. He was only thirty now. How had he made CEO of such a traditional company that fast?

Stupid question. Of course Jordan would be on the fast track, wherever he worked. He'd always been bright; his mind had attracted her teenage self just as much as his face. A man who could speak three other languages as fluently as his own; who knew all the European myths, not just the Greek and Roman ones; who knew Shakespeare even better than she did, back in the days when she still wanted to lecture on Renaissance drama. Dreams that had shattered and died, along with—

Alexandra pushed the thought away.

There was no way round it; she was going to have to be polite and shake his hand. She forced herself to keep her handshake brief, firm and businesslike and to ignore the tingles running along every nerve end as his skin touched hers. But then she made the mistake of looking into his eyes.

Midnight blue. Arresting. His eyes had caught her attention, the very first time she'd met him. Sweet seventeen and never been kissed. Until that night, when he'd seen beyond her image of the geeky girl with the mousy hair and glasses who didn't really fit in with everyone else at the party and had come over to talk to her. He'd danced with her. *Kissed her.*

She swallowed hard, and looked away, willing the memories to stay back.

She couldn't meet his eyes, Jordan noticed. Guilt? Not that it mattered, because as far as he was concerned she wasn't getting this job. No way was she going to be back into his life, not even in a work capacity. He'd get through this interview, and then he'd never have to set eyes on her again.

As the personnel manager, Harry was officially the one conducting the interview, so Jordan sat back and listened to him take Alexandra through the same questions he'd asked the others. Her answers were pretty much as he expected, so he glanced through her CV again. And then something stood out at him. The date she'd given for her A levels was three years after the date he remembered her being due to take them. Why? She'd been a straight-A student, the last person he'd expect to fail her exams.

Had the guilt of what she'd done finally hit her in the middle of her exams, so she'd messed them up? But, in that case, why had it taken her three years to retake them? And she didn't have the English degree he'd expected, either. She'd planned to become a lecturer, so why was she working in business instead of in an academic role?

He shook himself. It was none of his business, and he didn't want to know the answers.

He *really* didn't.

'Any questions?' Harry asked his colleagues.

Gina smiled. 'Not at this stage.'

And here was Jordan's opportunity to show everyone that Xandra Bennett was completely unsuitable. 'We did ask all the other candidates to prepare a presentation on how to take Field's forward,' he pointed out.

'But the agency added Xandra to the list at the very last minute,' Harry said, with a slight frown at Jordan. 'So it wouldn't be fair to expect her to give a presentation.'

'Not a formal presentation, of course,' Jordan agreed. 'But I do expect my senior staff to be able to think on their feet. So we'd like to hear your ideas, Ms Bennett. How would you see us taking Field's forward?'

Her eyes widened for a moment; she clearly knew that he was challenging her. And it was obvious that she also knew he was expecting her to fail.

Then she lifted her chin and gave him an absolutely glittering smile. The professional equivalent of making an extremely rude hand gesture. 'Of course, Mr Smith. Obviously, if this were a real situation, the first thing I'd ask is what the budget and the timescales are.'

She was the first person that day to mention budgets and timescales; the other candidates had just assumed. And some of them had assumed much more money than was available, talking about putting on TV spots in prime-time viewing. Completely unrealistic.

'And secondly I'd ask what you meant by taking Field's forward. Are you looking to attract a different customer base without losing the loyalty of your existing customers? Or do you want to offer your existing customers more services so they buy everything from Field's, rather than buy certain products and services from another supplier?'

Both Harry and Gina were sitting up a little straighter, clearly interested. She'd gone straight to the heart of their dilemma.

'What do you think?' Jordan asked.

'I'd start by doing an audit of your customers. Who they are, what they want, and what Field's isn't offering them now. And I'd talk to your staff. Do you have a staff suggestion scheme?'

'We used to,' Gina said.

'I'd reinstate it,' Alexandra said. 'Your staff know their products and their customers. They know what sells, what the seasonal trends are, and what their customers are looking for. They're the ones who are going to come up with the best suggestions for taking Field's forward—and I'd say that your marketing manager's job is to evaluate those suggestions, cost them, and work out which ones are going to have the most impact on sales.'

'Do you buy from us, Ms P—' Jordan had to correct himself swiftly '—Bennett?'

'No, I don't.'

That surprised him. He'd been so sure she'd claim to shop here all the time. She wasn't planning to curry favour that way, then. 'Why not?'

'Because as far as I can tell your range of clothes isn't targeted at my age group, the pharmacy chains have much better deals than you do on the perfume and make-up I buy, and I'm not in the market for fine crystal, silverware and porcelain dinner services,' she said.

Wow. She was the first of their candidates to criticise the store. And he could see that she'd taken Harry and Gina's breath away, too. 'So Field's is too traditional for you?' He couldn't resist needling her.

'Field's has one hundred and five years of tradition to look back on,' she said. 'Which should be a strength; being around for a long time shows your customers that they can rely on you. But it's also a weakness, because younger customers are going to see Field's as old-fashioned. As far as they're concerned, you sell nothing they'd be interested in. This is where their parents shop. Or even their grandparents. And you need to counteract that opinion.'

'So how would you raise their interest?' And, heaven help him, she'd already raised his own interest. Her comments were the best thing he'd heard all day. Her criticisms were completely constructive and she'd given solid reasons for her views. Reasons that he'd been thinking of, himself.

'Taking myself as a prospective customer—if you tempted me into the store by, say, a pop-up shop showcasing a hot new make-up brand I'm interested in, and you set it up next to my favourite designer's ready-to-wear range, then I'd realise that maybe I'd got the wrong idea about Field's. I'd be tempted to look around the store. If you sell what I want, at the right price, and your store loyalty scheme's good enough to tempt me away from my current supplier, then you'll get my business.'

He really couldn't fault that.

'And I'd also take a look at your online presence. Your website needs to be dynamic and involved with social media. Do you have an online community?'

'Not at the moment,' Gina said. 'How would you see one working?'

That was the moment that Alexandra really lit up. Suddenly she was shining, full of enthusiasm and bringing everyone along with her. 'Forums, hosted maybe by selected members of staff. Not all the time, just five minutes now and then. You could invite customers to be an expert in their field and share their tips. And you definitely need a plan for taking advantage of new media, if you're looking to attract a younger audience. Look at how they use social media and mobile media, and how you could make that work for Field's.' She rattled off a few examples—all practical ones.

Jordan glanced at her CV again. In her last job, she'd been responsible for online marketing, so she knew exactly what she was talking about. He made a mental note to look up her old company's website to see what she'd done there.

'Thank you, Ms Bennett. No further questions from me,' he said.

'Are there any questions you'd like to ask us?' Harry asked.

'Not at this stage,' Alexandra said with a smile. A polite smile, Jordan noticed, rather than a triumphant one; she clearly wasn't taking it for granted that her interview had gained her a ticket to the next round.

'Then thank you, Ms Bennett,' Gina said. 'If you'd like to wait outside for a couple of minutes?'

Jordan was aware of every single step Alexandra took as she crossed to the door. And, although he tried hard not to look, he couldn't help himself. Ten years ago, she'd been sweet and shy, her beauty hidden away; now, she was polished and confident, and any man with red blood in his veins would stand up a little straighter and try to catch her eye. He hated the fact that she could still make him react physically; so it was just as well he wouldn't have to see her again. Working with her would drive him crazy.

'She's by far and away the best of the bunch,' Harry said when Alexandra had closed the door behind her.

'Seconded,' Gina said. 'She understands our business a lot more than most of the others did. And she's got some great ideas.'

Which didn't leave Jordan any room to manoeuvre. If he hadn't known her in a previous life, he would've agreed with them. But he *had* known her. And that was a problem. Maybe that was the way round this. 'Unfortunately, I need to tell you there's a slight conflict of interest. One I wasn't aware of before the interview.'

Gina frowned. 'How do you mean?'

'I knew her. At school.' He coughed. 'Under a different name.'

Harry's eyebrows arched. 'Neither of you said a thing just now.'

Jordan knew he deserved the rebuke. Either or both of them could've acknowledged that they knew each other. But they hadn't. For exactly the same reason: one that he wasn't planning to share. He sighed. 'The middle of an interview's hardly the place for a reunion.' Not that he wanted a reunion with her. He'd moved on. And he didn't have any plans to go back.

'Her CV doesn't say she was at your school,' Harry pointed out.

'She wasn't at my school. I met her at a party—a friend of a friend of a friend. Actually, I was at university at the time.'

Harry shrugged. 'So you didn't know her *that* well.'

Well enough, Jordan thought, to make her pregnant. Except, when his mother had refused to pay her an extortionate allowance, she'd cold-bloodedly terminated their unborn child without even so much as discussing it with him. She hadn't even told him she was pregnant, and he couldn't forgive her for that.

And then she'd vanished to avoid any fallout. He'd spent weeks trying to find her, to no avail. When he'd finally tracked her down, he'd been gutted to discover that she was married…to someone else. He'd had to face how little he'd really meant to her—otherwise how could she have married another man so quickly after getting rid of his baby?

Not that he was going to tell Harry and Gina about that. It was something he never, ever talked about. To anyone. He'd buried the anger and the hurt, and they were staying buried.

'She's what we need,' Gina said. 'She can think on her feet, she's full of ideas, and she's straight-talking. And she was the only one to mention a budget—she's grounded in the real world.'

Jordan couldn't deny any of that. But could he cope with having her back in his life?

Harry clearly sensed the younger man's reservations, because he asked, 'Did you clash badly with her, or something?'

Or something. She'd been the first girl Jordan had really fallen in love with. She'd charmed him utterly. To the point where he'd even planned to spend the rest of his life with her.

How stupid he'd been. It would never have worked. Then again, neither had marrying someone he'd been friends with for years, someone who had the same kind of background that he did. He'd failed there, too. So, as far as he was concerned, relationships were best kept short and sweet—and ended before they started to sour.

'Jordan?'

He made a noncommittal murmur, not wanting to explain.

'Whatever happened—and I for one won't pry—you were both a lot younger then and still had a lot of growing up to do. People change,' Gina said.

Jordan didn't think so. Alexandra had been incredibly ambitious—expecting their unborn child to give her an entry into his world and a hand up from her own—and he'd bet that she was just the same, now. That kind of personality trait didn't change.

'Let's go through the candidates and see who we're going to bring back for a second interview,' he said, wanting to shift back onto safe ground.

On three of the final candidates, they were agreed; on

the fourth, there was no way he could explain why he didn't want her without dragging up too much of the past.

Just as they finished, Jordan's PA knocked on the door. 'I'm so sorry to interrupt, Mr Blake. I'm afraid it's a matter that can't wait,' she said to Harry.

'Go,' Jordan said. 'You too, Gina. I know you're both up to your eyes. I'll do the debriefs,' he said.

'Are you sure?' Harry asked.

'Absolutely.' It meant he'd get a word with her on his own—and then maybe he could find out what she was really up to.

As soon as his colleagues had gone, Jordan spoke to the candidates in the order he'd seen them. He commiserated with the ones who didn't get through to second interview and explained why, so they could work on their skills for the future; and he gave a briefing pack to the three candidates who'd got through to the next round.

And finally it was time to face Alexandra.

All the candidates had been seen in order. Most had come out looking dejected; three had come out looking pleased. And, as the last one to be interviewed, Alexandra was the last one to be debriefed.

She had thought about leaving quietly, so she didn't have to see the expression in Jordan's eyes when he told her that she was rejected. But that would be the coward's way out, and she wasn't a coward. Plus the debriefing was going to be useful for her next interview. Even so, her nerves were strung so tightly that she stumbled as she walked through the door.

'Ms…' He paused, looking her up and down. 'Bennett.'

Then she realised that Jordan was on his own. Oh, no. This was going to be really bad. He wouldn't have to hide the fact that he was gloating when he told her that she hadn't got the job.

Well, they did say that attack was the best form of defence. She lifted her chin. 'You could've just sent a message via the agency that I didn't get the job. You didn't need to bother telling me personally.'

'Actually, you made the list for second interview.' He handed her an envelope. 'And this is the briefing pack for the situation we want you to think about and discuss with us tomorrow.'

It was so unexpected that it silenced her. He was actually giving her a chance?

Then, when he spoke again, she wished she'd just said thank you and made a run for it.

'I wasn't expecting to see *you* today,' he said coolly.

'I had no idea you worked here.' Much less that he was the CEO.

He scoffed. 'Come off it. You know exactly who my family are.'

She frowned. 'No. All I knew was that they were posh.' In a different league from her own family. The ground floor of their entire house could've fitted into the Smiths' living room.

He didn't look as if he believed her. 'Let me refresh your memory. My great-grandfather started the store,' he said. 'My grandfather took over from him. And then my father.'

So it was his family business. 'And now you're the CEO. Following in their footsteps.' That much she could work out for herself. 'But it doesn't quite add up. Since it's a family business, why isn't your surname Field?'

He shrugged. 'It's my middle name. My father refused to change his surname when he married my mother.'

Oh. So the store belonged to his mother's family. With

a heritage like that, no wonder Vanessa Smith had been so confident. And maybe she could understand now why Vanessa had made that accusation when Alexandra had gone to her for help—an accusation that even now made a red mist swirl in front of Alexandra's eyes because it had been so unfair and so unjust.

Jordan looked at her. 'Speaking of names, I notice you've changed yours.'

Was that a roundabout way of asking her if she was married? Under employment law, he couldn't ask her; marital status was nothing to do with someone's performance in their job. On the other hand, it wouldn't hurt if he thought she was still married. Just in case he was under the very mistaken impression that she wanted anything from him other than this job. 'It's my married name.' And she'd kept it after the divorce.

'Even your first name's different,' he mused. 'I knew you as Alex.'

When she'd been a very different person. Naïve, believing that she'd been lucky enough to find her soul mate at the age of seventeen. Except she'd kissed her handsome prince and he'd turned into a slimy toad. She shrugged, affecting a cool she definitely didn't feel—even thinking about kissing when Jordan Smith was sitting right in front of her was a mistake. 'Xandra is a perfectly valid diminutive of Alexandra,' she said crisply.

'Very "marketing".'

Which was what her tutor had told her when she'd started doing the evening class. Look the part, sound the part, act the part, and you'll get the part. She'd followed that to the letter. 'Is that a problem?'

'No.' He paused. 'I told Harry and Gina I knew you.'

Knew her. Yeah. He'd known her, all right. In the Biblical sense. 'Didn't that put me out of the running?'

'They liked you.'

And he'd made it very clear that he didn't. Definitely guilt talking, she thought.

Meeting his gaze was a huge mistake. The man had proved to her years ago that he had no integrity where personal relationships were concerned. He'd abandoned her when she'd needed him most, let her down in the worst possible way. How could she possibly still find him in the slightest bit attractive? She reined her thoughts back in.

'If Field's were to offer you the job, would you take it?'

If that was his idea of an apology, Alexandra thought, it was much too little and much too late.

Then again, this was a real opportunity: to be the marketing manager of a traditional, well established department store, with a brief to bring it bang up to date. If she was offered the job, it'd be a real plus on her CV. If she turned it down just to spite him, she'd really be doing herself a disservice. 'I'd consider it,' she said.

'The job would mean working with me.'

'Is that a problem for you?'

He looked straight at her. 'Not if it's not a problem for you.'

In other words, it could work if they didn't talk about what had happened ten years ago. Could she do that, for the sake of her career?

She took a deep breath. 'That depends on what you offer me.'

Pretty much what she'd said to his mother.

Alexandra might look different and have a different name, but deep down she was still the same person. Still on the make. Jordan had to fight not to scowl at her and to keep his voice even. 'That depends,' he said, 'on what you can offer us. We'll see you here tomorrow at three.'

'I'll be here,' she said.

Yeah. And he'd just have to hope that this time she managed to show her true colours and put Harry and Gina off.

CHAPTER TWO

'SHE'S the one,' Harry said the following afternoon, when Alexandra left the room after her second interview. 'No question about it.'

'I really like her ideas for taking the store card to a new level, especially combining it with an app so customers can have instant access to all their account information wherever they are,' Gina added. 'And her presentation was flawless as well as enthusiastic. You'd never believe she only got the brief yesterday. She's going to be a real asset to Field's. The Board's going to love her.'

Jordan couldn't think of a single argument to change their minds. Mainly because they were right. Much as he hated to admit it, she *was* the best person for the job.

Maybe that huge ambition of hers could be harnessed to work in their favour.

Maybe.

Well, he'd never been a coward. He'd always stepped up to the mark, always shouldered his responsibilities. That wasn't going to change now. 'Let's call her in and give her the good news.'

The serious look on Jordan's face confirmed Alexandra's gut reaction. She hadn't got the job. Given that he was on the interview panel, that wasn't so surprising. Hopefully the debrief would tell her where she'd gone wrong; though she had a feeling that the real reason for her rejection lay ten years in the past.

What an idiot she'd been, putting herself in a position where he could reject her for a second time.

'Ms Bennett. Do sit down.'

She thought about defying him and remaining on her feet; but she was very glad she had taken the seat when he added, 'Welcome to the team.'

She'd got the job?

It surprised her so much that she was actually lost for words.

But her silence didn't seem to faze him. He continued, 'Mr Blake will sort out the details with you—when you're able to start, setting up an induction day so you can meet the rest of the team, sorting out your security for the store and the computer network.'

'Thank you.'

'Do you have any questions?' Harry asked.

'At the moment, only one.' She paused. 'Is the culture here always this formal? I'm more used to working on first-name terms.'

Jordan looked at her. So she was going to start challenging him already?

OK. He'd let her think she'd won this one, because it really wasn't an issue. 'No, it's not. Everyone here calls me Jordan.'

'Jordan,' she repeated.

It was the first time he'd heard her say his name in a decade, and he felt the colour rise through his face because he could remember a completely different tone to her voice, back then. When she'd cried out his name as she'd climaxed.

What an idiot he'd been. Not an issue, indeed; suddenly she'd made it one. And she hadn't just won this round, she'd completely flattened him. He needed to get out of here before he said something stupid. He glanced at his watch. 'I'm afraid I need to be somewhere. Excuse me. Thank you for your time, Ms B—Xandra.' He deliberately didn't meet her gaze and turned instead to the personnel manager. 'Harry, would you mind debriefing the other candidates?'

'Sure.'

Jordan walked out of the room without looking at her; when he reached his office he sank into his chair and closed his eyes. How the hell was he going to cope with having her back in his life?

Lots of cold showers, he answered his own question. And he'd better hope that the icy water would wake up his common sense. Because this particular woman was absolutely off limits, whatever his body might like to think.

A week later, Alexandra walked into Field's.

From today, this was *hers.* And she was going to take it from being a quiet, slightly old-fashioned department store to one that was buzzing. One that hit the news for all the right reasons. One that could deliver cutting-edge products, yet back them up with solid tradition.

And she could hardly wait.

She smiled as she swiped her store ID card through the slot by the staff entrance door, and stepped through.

Harry was there to meet her and introduced her to all the office staff, then took her round to meet the manager of each department. Jordan was conspicuous by his absence. She wasn't sure whether to be more relieved or cross; was he deliberately avoiding her? Well, he'd have to face her eventually, and she'd make sure that he didn't have a single thing to complain about. She was going to make a real success of this job.

A couple of days later, Jordan was doing his daily walkabout through the store—not so much checking up on his staff as making sure that he was visible rather than a faceless boss, and so he could see for himself if there were any issues that needed tackling or where his staff needed more support.

His body prickled with awareness and he glanced round. Alexandra—he still couldn't think of her as Xandra—was there, talking animatedly to the staff on one of the perfume counters. She was wearing another beautifully cut business suit that emphasised her curves and those high, high heels that made her legs look even longer.

As if she sensed him watching her, she glanced up and caught his gaze. She gave him a shy smile, and for a moment he was transported back to being nineteen years old, catching her gaze across a crowded party. She'd smiled like that at him back then, her brown eyes huge and slightly wary behind her spectacles.

And then she'd reeled him in. Hook, line and sinker.

He had to remember that. The shyness had been just an act, and she'd fooled him.

Though he was a fast learner. Nobody fooled him twice.

He gave her a cool, formal nod and turned away.

By the end of the week, Alexandra was absolutely certain that Jordan was avoiding her. He never seemed to visit the staff canteen—or, at least, not when she did; he hadn't dropped in to see how his newest manager was coping in the role, delegating that task to Harry; and he hadn't acknowledged her once on his daily walkabouts in the store, even though she knew damn well he'd seen her talking to customers and staff and setting up the customer audits.

Worse still, even when her back had been to him, her body seemed to have developed some kind of radar system that told her exactly where he was. And it was infuriating that she was still so aware of him.

If she was honest with herself, she knew the old attraction between them had never really gone away. But she'd just have to ignore it, because she didn't repeat her mistakes. Apart from the fact that Jordan Smith had been the second-biggest mistake of her life, her marriage had taught her just how rubbish her judgement was when it came to men. As far as she was concerned, from now on, she was married to her career. At least her career wasn't going to let her down or try to control her or make her feel bad about herself.

Though Jordan was the CEO here, and she was planning to make quite a few changes. Which meant that they were going to have to work together. They'd need to discuss her plans. Since he clearly wasn't going to make the first move and establish a decent working relationship between them, then she was going to have to be the one to do it. 'Stubborn, annoying, *ridiculous* man,' she muttered, and printed out the report she'd been working on.

It was late enough on a Friday evening for the rest of the office staff to have gone home, but she knew that Jordan would be working late. He put in a crazy number of hours—a work schedule that would strain just about any marriage to creaking point. Which wasn't her problem; she wasn't in the slightest bit interested in whether Jordan Smith was married and how happy he was. But his working habits did mean that she'd be able to talk to him this evening without anyone else being able to overhear.

Just in case it got awkward.

She walked down to the far end of the corridor—had he deliberately made sure that her office was as far away as possible from his? she wondered—and looked through the open door. He was seated at his desk, working at his computer. She'd never seen him wearing glasses before, and it made her catch her breath; right now he looked incredibly clever and incredibly sexy.

But she had to remember that she couldn't trust him as far as she could roll a ten-ton boulder up a slope.

OK, as a boss he seemed reasonable enough, and everyone she'd talked to in the department store had spontaneously mentioned what a nice guy he was and how he really cared about the staff; but when it came to personal stuff she knew he wasn't in the slightest bit reasonable or reliable. She had the physical scars to remind her. Scars that only a surgeon would see, but they were most definitely there. The physical ache had gone, but the emotional ache was something she'd learned to live with over the years.

She rapped on the door jamb.

He looked up, and his eyes widened in surprise. 'Is there something you need?'

'I just thought you might like to know what I've been working on for the last week.'

He shrugged. 'I don't believe in micromanagement. I know my managers are perfectly capable of doing their jobs.'

Ha. Considering he clearly hadn't wanted to give her the job in the first place, that was rich. 'Well, I'm telling you anyway, because I believe in good communications.' Neatly pointing out his own failings in that area, without actually saying the words. 'This is the stuff about the social media. It's a quick win and a small budget.' She walked over to his desk and handed him the report.

'You could've emailed this to me. Or given it to my PA.'

'So I could.' He wasn't even going to try meeting her halfway, was he? 'I'll remember that in future.' She gave him a cool smile and walked away.

Jordan almost called her back. Almost. But, until he'd managed to inure himself against those beautiful brown eyes, he needed to keep some distance between them.

Even so, instead of putting her report in his in-tray for later, he read through it.

There was a concise summary at the beginning, then each section had figures to back up her recommendations. She was definitely as bright as he remembered. And she was a team player: she'd acknowledged the input of every member of staff from the shop floor who'd made a suggestion. She'd suggested who would be good at hosting each of the community forums she'd recommended, and why. All the store's departments were included: home, garden, fashion, beauty, kitchen, technology, sport. She wanted sections on the website for articles giving 'how to' advice on everything from choosing lighting in a room or the right pillow for you through to make-up demonstrations and fashion tips, and she already had people in mind to write them or be filmed in action for a demonstration.

In one short week, she'd managed to spot the strengths of the team, and reinforce them. It was exactly as Harry and Gina had said: she'd be a real asset to the firm.

So why did he feel so antsy around her?

Not wanting to answer that question, he typed her a swift email instead. Headed 'Social media'.

I'll talk to the Board next week and recommend that they agree your plans. JS.

Nicely formal.

And now he could go back to what he'd been doing be-fore she'd torpedoed his concentration.

Easier said than done, Jordan thought wryly the follow-ing day, when he saw Alexandra balanced precariously on the top of a ladder in the toy department. She was stand-ing on *tiptoe,* for pity's sake. 'What do you think you're doing?' he demanded.

'Putting up a banner in the department to publicise the first story-time session, next week,' Alexandra said. 'What does it look like?'

'Dangerous, with a flagrant disregard for health and safety. You could hurt yourself, as well as customers or colleagues. Why didn't you ask Bill—or anyone taller than you, for that matter—to do it?'

'Bill was busy, and I wanted the banner up as soon as possible. The kids have worked hard on this.'

'Kids?' Jordan wasn't following.

'My friend Meggie's Year Two class.'

Meggie? He narrowed his eyes. He remembered Meggie. Alexandra's best friend. Ten years ago, she'd had great pleasure in telling him that Alexandra was married to someone who would treat her properly, and he could go and take a running jump. Or words to that effect. 'I see,' he said crisply.

But he noticed that the banner was composed of the words 'story time here Monday 10 a.m.', with each letter carefully cut out, painted and glued to the banner. And all around them were glued drawings of book covers, clearly the children's favourite books. The children had obviously worked really hard to make the banner bright and colour-ful. To make it special, for Alexandra.

Year Two. The children in the class would all be aged

seven. If things had been different, he and Alexandra might've had a child of their own in that class, as well as another in Year Five...

The thought made him snap at her. 'Will you get down from there before you fall?'

'I won't fall.'

In a suit and high heels? He wasn't going to take the risk. 'Get down,' he said again. 'I'll put the damn thing up for you.'

For a moment, he thought she was going to defy him, but then she shrugged. 'Fine. Thank you.'

He had to take his eyes off her legs as she descended from the ladder, carefully holding the banner.

Then she handed him one end. He'd just finished fixing it to the ceiling when he glanced down at her, and realised that she had a camera in her hands. 'What are you doing?'

'Taking shots for social media. To show that our CEO isn't afraid to get his hands dirty.'

'You're *photographing* me?'

'I'll let you vet the pictures, first.' She gave him a wicked grin. 'Maybe.'

Infuriating woman. He was about to say something cutting, when she asked, 'Would you mind putting the other end up for me, too, please, as you're here?'

After the fuss he'd made about her being up the ladder, he could hardly say no. He gave her a speaking look, but did so.

'My hero,' she purred.

'Don't push it,' he warned.

She just batted her eyelashes at him. And it made him want to grab her shoulders and...

Kiss her.

Shake her, he corrected himself. 'Don't take unnecessary risks again,' he said when he got down from the ladder.

'No, sir.' She gave him a smart salute.

He resisted the provocation, just, and stomped back to his office.

Later, his email pinged. The message contained a picture of him up the ladder, and a note from her.

Using this one. If I don't hear back within the hour, will assume OK.

He went straight to her office. 'How exactly are you intending to use that photograph?'

'Here.' She flicked into a screen on her computer and indicated the monitor so he could see the web page.

'What if I said no?'

'Let me see. This shows you as hands-on. All the mums are going to go weak at the knees and want to be here in case you walk by. All the grandmothers are going to think of their own sons and warm to you. The grandfathers will do the same, and the dads will see themselves in your shoes. So you're generating customer warmth. Plus you're creating links with the local community, as a local school worked on the banner—using material that Field's supplied. Now, why would you say no to that kind of PR?'

He didn't have an answer to that, because he knew she was right. 'Just stay inside health and safety guidelines in future,' he muttered.

She rolled her eyes. 'I'm not planning to have an accident and sue Field's or anything like that. I'm part of the team here. And I like being hands on.'

Hands on. He wished she hadn't used that phrase. He could still remember the feel of her hands against his skin. 'Whatever,' he said, annoyed by the fact that she could still unsettle him like that. 'If you'll excuse me. I have things that need sorting.' And he left her office before he did or said anything *really* rash.

On Monday morning, Jordan headed for the toy department. It was the first of their story-time sessions, and Alexandra had managed to get a minor children's TV presenter in to do the first one.

Except it seemed that the presenter had gone down with tonsillitis and wasn't able to appear. And Alexandra had stepped into the breach.

Jordan stood on the sidelines, watching her. She was sitting on a bean bag, with the children gathered round her and the mums sitting on chairs that looked as if they came from the staff canteen—no doubt she'd asked very nicely, with those huge eyes and the sweetest smile, and charmed the catering manager into helping. She was reading a rhyming story for the younger ones; some of them were clearly familiar with it, because she got them to join in on the chorus sections. She had a gorgeous voice, he thought, and he wasn't surprised that all the children were hanging onto every single word.

And then he found himself imagining her with their child. If she hadn't had the termination, would she have sat curled on the sofa with their toddler on her lap, pointing out the pictures and the words, gently teaching their little one to recognise letters?

Their child would've been ten, now. Nearly ready for high school. Would they have had a boy or a girl? And would they have had more children? A boy with his own dark hair and blue eyes, a girl with Alexandra's huge brown eyes and sunny smile…

Jordan was cross with himself for even thinking about it. It was pointless dwelling on what might have been, because you couldn't change the past. And right now children weren't part of his future in any case.

Quietly, without catching her eye, Jordan moved away. Alexandra was doing just fine on her own; she didn't need any support from him. And he wasn't going to crowd her.

Though he did return right at the end, just as Alexandra was finishing the story, with a camera.

She glanced up at him and for a moment he could see laughter in her eyes; she clearly recognised this as a bit of tit-for-tat. And he took more photographs of the line of children thanking her for the story and the queue of mums at the tills with books under their arms, before sliding the camera back into his jacket pocket and starting to stack the chairs.

'I saw that camera, you know,' she said, joining him in the chair-stacking.

'My marketing manager is very keen on social media and taking every photo opportunity we can,' he said.

'Good man. You're learning.' She patted his arm. 'Though I'm afraid we'll need to get all the mums to sign a release form before we can use those pics.'

Just as well there was a jacket sleeve and a shirt sleeve between his skin and hers. As it was, his skin was tingling where she'd touched him. How could she affect him like that, when he knew what he did about her?

He cleared his throat. 'I don't think anyone missed the TV presenter. You did a good job.'

'Thank you. I'm getting the staff to do a rota; they're all going to read their favourite stories.' She smiled. 'It's lovely that everyone in the store wants to get involved, whether they're from the shop floor or behind the scenes. Maureen from the canteen's even coming in on her day off to read her granddaughter's favourite story.'

'Was that a hint that you're expecting me to read a story?' he asked.

'Could be.'

She smiled again, and he noticed the dimple in her cheek. Cute. How had he forgotten that? And it really made him want to touch it. Touch *her*. Dip his head and brush his mouth against hers. Kiss her until they were both dizzy.

'Jordan?'

'Uh—sorry.' He felt the colour rise in his cheeks. She'd just caught him staring at her like a fool. 'You know me. Mind always on the next project.'

'I said, it might be a hint. If you want to read a story for the kids, that is. If you're not too busy.'

'I'll think about it.' Again, he found his thoughts coming back to the baby. Did she ever think about their baby? Did she ever regret what she'd done? Did she ever wonder what it might've been like, making a family with him?

And just what was wrong with him, suddenly thinking about having a family? Since the break-up of his marriage, he'd pushed all that sort of thing to the back of his mind and concentrated on making Field's the best department store he could.

'What made you think about having story time sessions?' he asked. 'Did your parents used to read to you a lot, or something?'

She shook her head. 'It was Miss Shields, my primary school teacher. She used to read a few pages to us just before we went home. And she took me off the official school reading scheme and lent me books that I enjoyed a lot more.'

He should've guessed it hadn't been her parents to encourage her love of reading. She'd told him once that she was the first person in her family to stay on for A-levels, let alone think about going to university.

'How about you? Did your parents read to you?' she asked.

'I had a story every night.' From his nanny. His parents had been busy at work; they hadn't had the time to read to him.

'And you read to your own children?'

'I don't have children.' Except the one he hadn't known about—the one who hadn't even been born. He knew he shouldn't ask, because he really didn't want to hear the answer, but he couldn't help the question. 'You were pretty good at that. I assume you read to yours?'

For just a second, he could've sworn that she flinched. And she turned away as she said, 'I read to my godchildren. Meggie's two.'

So she still didn't have children. Then again, pregnancy would make her face up to what she'd done when she was eighteen. And he was beginning to think that maybe Alexandra was a bit less hard-boiled than he'd believed her to be. How did she feel about the prospect of starting a new family, knowing that she'd deliberately chosen not to have a family before?

'Excuse me. I'm sure you're busy and I need to get some things sorted here. Thanks for your help in stacking the chairs.' And then she fled.

CHAPTER THREE

But Jordan couldn't stop thinking about it all evening. Thinking about *her*. Alexandra still didn't have children. Why? Was it the guilt about what she'd done to his baby stopping her, or had her husband not wanted children anyway?

Her husband.

The words dropped into his thoughts like a clanging bell. Alexandra was married. Jordan didn't believe in cheating. And, even if she hadn't been married, she worked with him. How many times had he seen an office romance end in tears? And then there was the kicker: been there, done that and she'd destroyed his trust. Never again.

No, what he needed to do now was to establish a working relationship with her; maybe then he could move on and leave the demons of the past behind, locked away where they belonged.

On Tuesday night, Jordan was working late as usual. He went to make himself a cup of coffee in the staff kitchen, and noticed the light shining through Alexandra's open door at the far end of the corridor. She was working late again, too. Now he thought about it, she'd worked late every night since she'd started. Was she trying to prove herself to him? Or was she struggling with her workload, unable to cope with the demands of the job?

He walked down the corridor, knocked on her open door and leaned against the door jamb. 'Won't Mr Bennett have something to say about you working this late every night?'

She looked up and simply shrugged.

She was so ambitious that she'd put her job before her marriage? he thought, stunned.

Then she gave him a cool look. 'Won't Mrs Smith have something to say about *you* working this late?'

'Touché.' He gave her a wry smile. 'Actually, I didn't come in to fight with you, just to say that I was making coffee and to ask if you wanted a mug, too. And, for the record, I don't expect my staff to work the same hours as I do.'

'I'm fine. I'm just settling in and enjoying the challenges of my new job.' But she returned his smile, her expression softening slightly. 'Sorry, I didn't mean to snap at you just then.' She glanced down at her left hand. The ring finger was defiantly bare. How hadn't he noticed that before? 'I guess I should tell you that there isn't a Mr Bennett. Well, there is,' she amended, 'but he's not married to me any more. I just kept his name.'

She was single?

For a moment, he forgot to breathe.

Oh, for pity's sake. That wasn't what this was meant to be about. He was simply trying to set up a decent working relationship between them. And maybe he should offer her the same honesty. 'There isn't a Mrs Smith, either,' he admitted. 'She went back to her maiden name after the divorce.' And then she'd remarried.

'I'm sorry it didn't work out for you.'

'And you.'

It was the most civil they'd been towards each other

since she'd walked back into his life, and Jordan was surprised at how good it felt.

The harsh overhead light showed that there were shadows under her eyes. He remembered her looking like that
years ago, when she'd been studying too hard. 'When was
the last time you ate?' he asked.

She blinked, looking surprised. 'What?'

'It's nearly eight o'clock. You've been here for more than
twelve hours. Did you actually have a lunch break today?'

'Yes.'

Though the slight hesitation in her voice told him the
truth. 'It was a sandwich at your desk while you were
working, wasn't it?'

She spread her hands. 'Busted. But there's just not
enough time for lunch. There's so much I want to do.'

He knew that, from the wish list she'd emailed him.
Pop-up shops, chosen by the consumer through an online poll; a Christmas bazaar showcasing local craftspeo-
ple, held in a marquee in the courtyard café; an events
programme including demonstrations that would also be
broadcast on the Internet; and a dozen more ideas, some
of them completely off the wall but he had a feeling that
she could make them work. No, she wasn't struggling with
her job. She was struggling with prioritising things—and
only because she'd had so many good ideas. He'd be doing
the same, in her shoes.

'If you don't pace yourself properly, you'll burn out,'
he warned.

Her expression said very clearly, *Right, as if you give
a damn about that.*

'Actually, I do give a damn,' he said. 'We look after our
staff at Field's.'

'Everyone I've spoken to is happy.'

That was completely out of left field. He blinked. 'You asked my staff if they were happy?'

'No, that wasn't my brief. But I can tell they're happy by the way they talk. They're enthusiastic, they're full of ideas, and they love the new staff suggestion scheme. You should see my inbox.'

'Why don't you tell me about it over dinner?'

'Dinner?'

He pushed aside thoughts of damask tablecloths and the light from vanilla-scented candles glinting on antique silver cutlery. This was a working relationship; they weren't picking up where they'd left off, before she'd vanished. Before the bombshells had dropped. 'I have to eat. So do you. We might as well eat together while we discuss it.'

She shrugged. 'I was going to stop in ten minutes anyway. I was going home to make myself an omelette.'

'An omelette's fine by me.'

Her eyes narrowed. 'I don't remember inviting you back.'

He blew out a breath. 'Sorry. That was pushy. How about a compromise?' he asked. 'There's this trattoria just round the corner. It's pretty basic, but the food's excellent.'

She leaned back in her chair, eyes narrowing even further as she stared at him. 'You're asking me out to dinner?'

'A *working* dinner,' he clarified. 'To make up for the fact that I haven't had a chance to spend any real time discussing your ideas with you.'

They both knew that wasn't what he was really saying. He'd been avoiding her, and they were both well aware of the fact.

'So you'll listen to my ideas.'

'And give you feedback. Yes.'

Her expression showed that she was considering it.

Weighing up the pros and cons. So she was just as wary of him as he was of her, then. Guilt talking? he wondered.

'OK,' she said eventually.

'How long will it take you to get ready?'

'As long as it takes to back up my files and shut down the computer.'

Ha. Well, of course she wasn't going to change, or re-touch her make-up, or spritz herself with perfume. This wasn't a date. It was simply discussing work while they ate. Multi-tasking.

'Meet you back here in ten minutes?' he suggested.

'Sure.'

Ten minutes later, when he met her outside her office, he was pretty sure that she'd reapplied her lipstick, but he didn't make a comment. He simply ushered her out of the store and down the side street to the little trattoria he'd discovered a couple of years before.

'Red or white?' he asked as the waiter arrived to take their drinks order.

She shrugged. 'I don't mind. Though I would like some water as well, please. Still, with ice.'

He remembered her preferring white wine; her tastes might have changed over the years, but he decided to play safe and ordered a bottle of pinot grigio and a jug of water. 'Thanks, Giorgio.'

'*Prego,* Jordan.' The waiter smiled back at him.

'If the waiter's on first-name terms with you, I assume you eat here a lot?' she asked.

Jordan shrugged. 'It's convenient. And, actually, he's the owner. His wife's the cook.'

She gave him a sidelong look. 'So you haven't actually learned to cook, yet?'

He knew what she was referring to. The time he'd taken her back to his place when his parents had been out. He'd

put some bread under the grill to toast—and then he'd
started kissing her on the sofa and forgotten all about the
toast until the smoke detector had started shrieking. He
couldn't remember how to turn the alarm off, so they'd
had to flap a wet towel underneath it and open all the windows; even then, the house had reeked of burnt toast for a
whole day afterwards.

'It's convenient,' he repeated. After Lindsey had left
him for someone who didn't have workaholic tendencies,
he'd discovered that he really didn't enjoy cooking a meal
for one, even if it was just shoving a ready meal in the microwave. He tended to eat at lunchtime in the staff canteen,
then grabbed a sandwich at his desk in the evening; and
on days when he didn't have time for lunch, he grabbed a
sandwich on the run and ate at the trattoria after work.

'What do you recommend?' she asked, glancing over
the edge of the menu at him.

'Pretty much everything on the menu. Though the lasagne's particularly good,' he said.

'Lasagne it is, then. Thank you.'

He ordered the same for both of them when Giorgio
returned with the wine and water. 'Bread and olives?'
Giorgio asked.

He glanced at Alexandra. At her nod, he smiled. 'Yes,
please.'

If anyone had told Alexandra six months ago that she'd
be having dinner with Jordan Smith, and enjoying it, she
would've laughed. Really, really scornfully.

But Jordan was excellent company. Charming, with
good manners. And she was actually having a good time.

Then she reached for another piece of the excellent bread
at the same time as he did; when their fingers touched, her
mouth went dry. Oh, hell. She could remember him touch-

ing her much more intimately, and it sent a shiver of pure lust through her.

She mumbled an apology and withdrew, waiting for him to tear off a piece of bread before she dared go anywhere near the bread basket again.

'The bread's good,' she said, hoping to cover up the awkwardness—and hoping even more that he wouldn't guess what she'd just been thinking about.

He raised an eyebrow. 'I did wonder if you'd stick to just the olives.'

'Why?' For a moment, she looked puzzled. 'Oh. Because of the carbs.' She gave him a wry smile. 'You're obviously used to dating twig-like women who exist on a single lettuce leaf—and maybe a nibble of celery if it's a special night out.'

'I don't date twig-like women.' He couldn't help the slight snap in his voice. It was none of her business who he dated.

'Another elephant,' she said softly. 'At this rate, we're going to have a whole herd.'

'How do you mean?'

'The elephant in the room. Screened off. Things we don't talk about, things that are absolutely off limits. The past. Your marriage. Mine. The women you date who don't eat.' Her gaze held his. 'Would you like to add any more to the herd?'

He really hadn't expected this. 'That's very direct.'

'I find it's the easiest way. It cuts out the lies.'

Was she admitting that she was a liar? Or was she accusing *him* of being a liar? Right at that moment, he couldn't tell. But he wasn't the one who'd behaved badly. He wasn't the one who didn't even bother to say, 'You're dumped,' but simply went incommunicado. Then, when he'd heard what his mother had to say about the situation and tried to find out what the hell was going on, Alexandra had simply vanished. He hadn't been able to find her and drag the truth out of her.

'By my reckoning,' she continued, 'that leaves us the weather, work or celebrity gossip as our next topic of conversation. Would you like to choose?'

There was the slightest, slightest glint of laughter in her eyes, and suddenly the tension in his spine drained away. 'Work, I think,' he said. 'Before we have a fight.'

She inclined her head in recognition. 'That's direct, too.'

'Yeah.' He couldn't bring himself to echo her words back at her. Because she was the one who'd told the lies; and they'd just tacitly agreed not to discuss it. He still wanted to know why—why hadn't she told him about the baby? Had she ever loved him, or had his mother been right and she'd just seen him as a meal ticket for life? But he wasn't sure he was going to be able to handle the answers to his questions; and anyway, whatever had happened in the past, right now he knew that Alexandra Bennett was going to be really good for Field's. And his family business was the whole purpose of his life nowadays.

'Tell me about your ideas,' he said instead, then sat back and watched her blossom as she talked. As she expounded on her ideas her eyes shone and her face was completely animated. She clearly loved her job; this was her passion, the reason she got up in the mornings.

And then he wished that word hadn't slipped into his head. Passion. He could remember her being passionate in bed with him, once she'd got past her shyness. Once she'd got past the embarrassment and awkwardness of her very first time, started to learn how she liked him to touch her, and what gave him the most pleasure when she touched him…

Oh, hell, he really needed to stop letting his thoughts run away with him like this.

'So why did you pick marketing?' he asked.

She blinked. 'Sorry?'

'I thought you were going to be a lecturer.'

'That's not relevant.'

And he'd hit a nerve, judging by the expression on her face. 'OK. Ignore that. I just wondered what made you pick marketing as a career?'

She shrugged. 'I was in a bit of a rut in my job. A friend who worked in HR persuaded me to let her practise on me and got me to do some tests. The results said that marketing would suit me as a career, so I found myself a job as a marketing assistant and started studying for my professional exams.'

Exams, he remembered from her CV, where she'd gained distinctions in every paper. And she'd done the whole lot in less than a year. 'So was your friend right? Are you happy?'

'Yes. And this job is a challenge. I'm glad I went for it.' She paused. 'Though I really didn't know you were anything to do with Field's.'

Her eyes were very clear; maybe she was telling the truth.

'The agency put you in at the very last minute.'

'I'd just signed up with them. I was looking to make my next career move,' she explained. 'They said there was the perfect job for me, except the application date had already passed. And then they said they'd see if they could do something about it.' She spread her hands. 'I really wasn't expecting them to ring me and say I'd got an interview, so I didn't bother doing any research on Field's. When they said I had an hour and a half to get there, it was too late to do more than read the factsheet they sent me and then spend five minutes walking round the store before the interview.'

He couldn't leave it. 'If you'd known I was going to be doing the interview, would you have turned up?'

'I don't know,' she said. 'I would've had to think very hard about it.'

'But you came back for a second interview.'

'Because I wanted the job. This sort of challenge doesn't come up that often, and I realised it'd be pointless cutting off my nose to spite my face.'

He could appreciate that.

'So why did you give me the job?' she asked.

Even though he hadn't wanted her back in his life? 'Fair question,' he acknowledged. 'Because you were the best candidate. And you said it wouldn't be a problem working with me.'

'It won't be.'

He wasn't so sure. 'This elephant in the corner thing isn't going to work. We're better off getting everything out of the way. We need to talk about what happened. And then we can move on and have a chance of a decent working relationship.'

Her face went white. 'You want to talk about it *here?*'

She had a point. The trattoria was quiet, but not that quiet. 'After we've eaten,' he conceded. 'Your place or mine?'

She shook her head. 'Neutral territory. Isn't there a park or something near here?'

'On a March evening? We'll freeze. Your place or mine?' he repeated inexorably.

She sighed. 'Yours.'

So she could walk out when it got too much for her? he thought cynically. 'That's settled, then.'

The lasagne was good. Probably the best she'd ever tasted. Except Alexandra was so nervous, she could barely swallow. Why hadn't she kept her mouth shut? Why had she had to make that stupid comment about him dating twig-like women? Why hadn't she kept the conversation strictly to business and insisted on discussing marketing ideas for the department store?

She really didn't want to drag up the past. To rip the top off her scars and let all the pain come flooding back. She'd reinvented herself, worked hard to make something of her life.

But maybe he was right. Maybe they did need to get all this out of the way. And in some respects it would be good to have closure. To hear him apologise, even though it was way too late and nothing could fix what had happened.

She toyed with her food.

'Don't you like it?' Jordan asked.

'I do. I've just...' She might as well be honest with him. 'I've lost my appetite.'

He blew out a breath. 'My fault.'

'Yeah.' There was no point in telling fibs.

'OK. I'll get the bill.'

She frowned. 'You haven't eaten your own meal.'

He shrugged. 'I'm not that hungry any more, either.' For the same reason as her. He wasn't looking forward to their conversation. But it had to be done. Like lancing a boil. Letting the poison out.

She took a couple of notes from her purse and handed them to him. 'My half of the bill.'

'Not necessary. I think I can just about afford to buy my marketing manager a meal.'

She shook her head. 'I don't like being beholden to anyone. This was business.' At least, they'd planned to talk business. Even though in the end they hadn't ended up talking about any of her ideas. She lifted her chin. 'So I'm paying my share. It's not up for discussion.'

For a moment, she thought he was going to argue. But then he shrugged. 'OK. Purely to keep the peace.'

A peace they were both about to destroy, she thought wryly.

'Do you have a problem with me ordering us a taxi?' he asked.

'No.'

'Good.'

The silence between them as they waited for the taxi was painful; it was a relief when the car arrived. Though the silence in the taxi was just as bad. She wasn't willing to break it by chattering about something inconsequential; when she stole a sidelong glance at him, there were tense lines around his mouth, so he clearly felt the same.

By the time the driver pulled up outside the building where Jordan lived in Notting Hill, Alexandra felt as brittle as the most delicate glass. One wrong touch, and she'd shatter.

He tapped in a code to let them into the lobby. Ushered her into the lift with a gesture. Unlocked the front door to his flat and motioned with his hand for her to walk inside.

'Coffee?' he asked as he closed his front door behind them.

It would've choked her. 'No, thanks.'

'Come and sit down.'

His flat was just as she'd expected. Masculine, plain— and everything was utterly luxurious. Carpet deep enough to sink into, making her feel guilty that she hadn't re- moved her shoes; cream leather sofas that were incredibly soft to the touch; and state-of-the-art television and audio equipment.

Without comment, she sat on the sofa, and was relieved when he took the chair opposite her rather than sitting next to her. If they were going to get through this, she didn't want him too close. Didn't want him distracting her.

'So,' he said. 'Time to talk.'

And she had no intention of letting him take the upper hand. She lifted her chin. 'So you're finally going to tell me why you cheated on me?'

CHAPTER FOUR

JORDAN looked as if she'd just poleaxed him. He sat down and stared at her in what looked like utter incomprehension. 'I *what?*'

'You cheated on me,' Alexandra repeated.

He shook his head. 'No, I didn't. Why on earth would you think I'd do something like that?'

'Even if I hadn't been told outright, I could see the signs.' She folded her arms. 'You weren't that serious about me—you were just messing about with me until Miss Right came along, weren't you?'

He frowned. 'I don't get any of this. What do you mean, told outright? And I wasn't messing about with you.'

'Jordan, you never rang me in term time. You never came back to see me, or invited me to come down to Oxford for the weekend.'

'You *know* why. The terms at Oxford are short and intense. I was studying all the time and I had tutorials on Saturday mornings. I wanted a Double First, and that meant putting in the work. I barely had time to breathe.'

'Would it have killed you to text me? To email me? To let me know you were thinking of me?'

His frown deepened. 'I don't remember any of this being an issue at the time. You were studying for your exams and I was studying for mine. If you weren't happy with the way things were, why didn't you say?'

'Because I was scared I'd push you away,' she said. 'Or that you'd laugh at me. I mean, my background was nothing like yours.'

His face tightened. 'So now you're saying I'm a snob?'

'No. I'm saying I was eighteen, I wasn't exactly confident in myself back then, and I'd seen my best friend messed about by someone who went away to study, wasn't faithful to her and left her struggling as a single mum. So, yes, I worried that it'd be like that with you. That it'd be a case of out of sight, out of mind, and you'd find someone else.'

He shook his head. 'That's completely unfair. Not all men are the same.'

'I know that. But what happened to Meggie made me wonder. Would things change between us when you were at Oxford and I was still at home? Would you meet someone else while you were away, someone more suitable, and dump me?'

'I'm still not following. What do you mean, more suitable?'

'You never let me meet your family, we never hung out with your friends when you came home, and part of me wondered, why on earth would someone like you date someone like me—someone who wasn't from your world and would never fit in?'

'Of course you'd fit in. And I didn't keep you away from my family on purpose. My friends, yes, purely because I didn't want to have to share the time I had with you. If anything, I neglected them for you. But I never kept you away from my family. My parents worked long hours; they weren't home that much. That's the only reason you didn't get to meet them properly.' He stared at her. 'I still can't believe you thought I cheated on you. So who said I did? Meggie?'

'No. A woman who said she was your girlfriend.' Alexandra took a deep breath. 'I called you at Oxford, and a woman answered your phone. I asked to speak to you, and she asked who I was. And then she made it very clear that she wasn't happy about some random woman phoning up her boyfriend.'

'I don't have the faintest idea what you're talking about. *Who* you're talking about. What was her name?'

'I didn't ask. I wasn't exactly thinking straight,' she admitted.

'You're telling me! Alex, you knew I lived out in my second year. I shared a house with four other students. People were always just dropping in. And, just because some girl answered my phone, you assumed I was cheating on you?' He shook his head. 'That's incredibly unfair.'

And childish. The implication stung. 'I didn't assume anything. It's what she *said*. That she'd left you in the shower and had come downstairs to make coffee for you both. She made it very obvious that you'd just had sex. And she told me not to ring you again.'

'I didn't have sex with anyone in Oxford when I was seeing you. Not in the shower or anywhere else.' He raked his hand through his hair. 'How could you believe something that a complete stranger told you—someone whose name you didn't even know?'

'Remember I was eighteen, Jordan. And I was panicking.' She'd been full of self-doubt and raging hormones, worrying about what he'd say when she told him the news that she was pregnant. Worrying that he'd dump her, the way Meggie's boyfriend had dumped her when she'd told him about their baby.

'So is that why you didn't tell me about the baby?'

'No.' She wrapped her arms round herself. 'That's why I rang you in the first place. To tell you about the baby. I tried to wait until you were home for the holidays and not disrupt your studies, but I just couldn't. What was happening—it was too big for me to deal with on my own. I needed to talk to you. And then, when I thought you had another girlfriend in Oxford...' She could still remember how she'd felt. Dismayed. Shocked. The way the hurt had seeped through her, numbing her. 'I didn't see that there was any point in telling you about the baby after that, because I didn't think you'd want to know. And it wasn't as if you called me back.'

'I didn't call you back because I had no idea that you'd phoned in the first place. Nobody gave me a message that you'd tried to get hold of me. You weren't even shown on my phone as the last caller.'

'But I must've been. Unless...' A nasty thought struck her. 'Maybe she deleted the record from your call log. To cover her tracks. Because if you'd called me back, I would've had a fit about you cheating on me with her.'

'And then I would've told you the truth—that I was doing nothing of the kind.' He stared at her. 'But obviously you thought I didn't call you back because I didn't want to.'

'What else was I supposed to think? I'd called you, and you didn't call me back.'

'Whoever that woman was, I wasn't sleeping with her.' He looked awkward. 'I admit, I had offers. There was one particular girl who threw herself at me a few times, but I turned her down. I told her I had a girlfriend at home and I wasn't interested. She still hung around our house a bit too much.' He shook his head. 'I can't even remember her name now. It was ten years ago. But I most definitely didn't have any kind of relationship with her, or anyone else, while I was seeing you.'

Looking at him now, she believed him. He hadn't been cheating on her. All these years, she'd believed a pack of lies from someone who'd clearly tried to manipulate her way into Jordan's life and make sure his real girlfriend stayed out. Alexandra had been so mixed up, full of hormones; the woman's lies had been so close to her own fears and doubts that she hadn't questioned them. She bit her lip. 'I know it's a bit late, now—but I'm sorry. I should've believed in you. I should've called you again instead of thinking the worst of you and backing off.'

'As you said, you were eighteen and you weren't particularly confident. You were so shy when I first met you—so, yes, I can understand that.' His expression hardened. 'But what I really can't understand is why you did what you did next.'

It was her turn to frown. 'How do you mean?'

'You didn't tell me about the baby—but you told my mother.'

'Because I thought she might help me.'

His lip curled. 'Don't you mean, pay you?'

'*Pay* me?' She stared at him. 'I don't understand.'

'You asked her for money. And when she wouldn't give you anything, you decided to dump me—without even bothering to tell me—and had a termination.'

He'd thought *that* of her? Alexandra was too shocked to say anything at first. And then anger flooded through her. Yes, she'd been wrong about him—but he'd been far more wrong about her. 'You bastard.'

'I'm just telling it like it is.'

'No. Absolutely not.' She shook her head emphatically. 'How could you possibly believe I'd ever do something like that?'

'Let's see.' His face was grim. 'When I got back from Oxford, my mother said that you'd told her you were pregnant with my baby and you asked her for money. True, or not true?'

'True,' she muttered.

'So I tried ringing you, but your mobile phone was permanently switched off. I couldn't get hold of you. I went to see your parents, and they told me you didn't live there any more. I asked about the baby, and they told me you were no longer pregnant. They made it clear I wasn't welcome. So then I got in touch with Meggie, thinking she'd tell me where you were—and she said you didn't want to see me ever again.'

Alexandra was shaking. How, how, *how* could he have put the pieces together and got the picture so wrong?

'Well? Isn't that what happened, Alex?'

'Not like the way you're making out it happened. Yes, I told your mother about the baby and I asked her to help me. I needed money for nursery fees, so I could still go on to do my degree and know the baby was being looked after properly while I was studying.' Back then, she'd still thought she could do it. Go to university, take her degree, then teach; and she'd manage to support their baby on her own, once she'd graduated. 'She refused. And yes, I left home. And yes, I wasn't pregnant any more when I left home. And yes, I told Meggie and my parents I never wanted to see you again. I hated you, Jordan, because when I needed you most you just weren't there. All of that's true.' She lifted her chin. 'But I didn't have a termination. I had an ectopic pregnancy.'

'You had a what?' He stared at her, looking completely confused.

'An ectopic pregnancy. It's where the egg gets stuck in the Fallopian tube and grows there instead of in the womb,' she explained. Just as the doctor had explained it to her, all those years ago. The reason why she'd been in such agony. 'You don't know it's happened until the foetus grows big enough. Then the tube ruptures.' She swallowed hard. 'I guess it hurts a bit.'

Horror filled his expression. 'Oh, my God. Alex.' He stood up and moved to wrap his arms round her, but she lifted her hands to tell him to back off.

'Don't touch me, Jordan.' The full impact of his words had just sunk in. He'd thought she'd used their baby as a bargaining ticket to get money—and that, when she failed, she'd deliberately had an abortion. Did he think she'd deliberately got pregnant, too? That she was the gold-digger his mother had accused her of being? 'I know we didn't plan to have a baby, but I can't believe you thought I'd ever have a termination. That I'd get rid of our baby without a second thought. I loved you so much, and you let me down. I didn't think you could let me down any more than you did back then…but you just have.' She felt sick.

'What was I supposed to think, Alex? I had to find out about our baby from someone else—and then I was told that there was no baby any more. You vanished. Nobody knew where you'd gone—or, if they did, they weren't going to tell me—and I couldn't find you. I couldn't get in touch with you to find out your side of things.'

'I couldn't bear to be at home, not afterwards. My parents…they couldn't see why I was so upset about losing the baby. The way they saw it, with me losing the baby, the problems had all been solved. There was no baby to get in the way of me doing my exams and going to university.' She drew her knees up and wrapped her arms round them. 'I hated the fact they were relieved. Every day, it hurt more. I couldn't bear it. So I left home.'

'Where did you go?' he asked.

'A hostel, for the first few days. I stuck it out for nearly a week, but I hated not having any privacy. Though I had some savings.' She shrugged. 'And I knew I wasn't going to university any more, so I thought I might as well use them. I scoured all the small ads and managed to find myself a bedsit.' She grimaced. 'It was damp. There was this huge patch of black mould on the ceiling and I couldn't get rid of the smell, but even so it was better than the hostel. It was mine.'

Jordan hated to think of her struggling like that, living in a damp, poky bedsit. Even his student house in his second year had been dry, clean and spacious, thanks to the generous allowance his parents had given him.

'And I found a job so I could support myself. It was fine as long as I could do a bit of overtime.'

No, it wasn't fine at all. She should've been enjoying her life as a student, the way she'd planned, not working all hours to make ends meet. Her life had been turned upside down—and his had been endless privilege. There was nothing he could say, nothing he could do. He couldn't even put his arms round her now to comfort her, because her body language was screaming 'keep away'—and anyway it was ten years too late.

He'd never felt so helpless, so useless, in his entire life.

'What made you think you couldn't still go to university?' he asked, focusing on the one bit he didn't quite understand.

'I knew I hadn't got the grades. I missed three papers while I was in hospital, and I was on so many painkillers for the next couple of days that I couldn't think straight. I have no idea what I wrote in my exams, but I'm pretty sure it was garbage.' She shrugged. 'I knew I'd blown it and my dreams had gone, so what was the point of waiting for my results to confirm it? So I left home the day after my last exam.'

When she still hadn't recovered physically from losing the baby, let alone dealt with the emotional pain. He hated to think that she'd been so alone. 'I understand why you wanted some space from your parents, but why Meggie? I mean, she was your best friend and she'd been through… well, something similar. Couldn't you have stayed with her for a bit?'

Alexandra shook her head. 'I couldn't bear seeing the pity in her eyes every time she looked at me. I'm not proud of myself, but I cut myself off from her as well. Until I got my head together again.'

Or so she'd thought at the time. She'd been swept off her feet by Nathan Bennett, and then—filled with delight when he'd placed the diamond ring on her finger—had phoned Meggie, wanting to share the news with her best friend, apologise for going AWOL and asking Meggie to be her bridesmaid. She'd had no idea that she'd gone from the frying pan straight into the fire.

'Alex, if I'd known…' He looked tortured.

'But you *did*,' she said. 'That's the whole point. You knew. I collapsed at school, the day after my first exam. They called an ambulance; my mum and dad came to the hospital and I begged them to get hold of you. I gave them your number—your parents' number as well as your mobile. Dad went to phone you. Then he came back and told me you wouldn't come.'

He frowned. 'I never spoke to your parents.'

'So you're saying they lied to me?'

'You're saying my mother lied to me?' he countered.

'Your mother twisted things. She said there was no way I could prove the baby was yours, and she wasn't going to let me foist it on you and ruin your life. And I was a cheap little gold-digger who saw you as a meal ticket for life, but I was mistaken because she wasn't going to give me a penny.' She shivered. 'It wasn't like that. I loved you. And it *was* your baby.'

At least he didn't try to deny that.

She dragged in a breath. 'I didn't ask her to pay me off, Jordan. I asked her to give me a loan, because I knew my parents couldn't afford to help me. I was going to pay her back once I'd graduated and had a job.'

'That's not what she told me. She just said you asked for money.'

'Technically, I did ask for money.'

'But not in the way she made me think you did. Oh, hell.' He closed his eyes briefly, as if shutting out the pain, then stared at her. 'Alex, I'm so, so sorry. If I'd had any idea…The second she told me about the baby, I came to see you and find out what was going on.' He paused. 'Your parents didn't say you'd been in the emergency department and lost the baby. They just said you weren't pregnant any more.'

'And you assumed that I'd got rid of the baby deliberately.' She shook her head in disgust. 'I can't believe you'd think that of me.'

'What can I say? I was twenty years old and I still had a lot of growing up to do. Alex, all I knew is that you were pregnant with our baby, and then you weren't, and you didn't want anything to do with me. You hadn't told me *anything*. I was furious with you. I thought you'd dumped me without even bothering to tell me that you wanted to end it—and that's why I believed the worst of you.' He dragged in a breath. 'I guess it was easier than digging to find out the truth. And I'm sorry. I'm sorry I was such an arrogant bastard who didn't think any further than his own ego. I'm sorry I wasn't there for you.' He came to kneel in front of her chair and placed his hand over hers. 'If I'd known about the baby earlier, believe me, I would've been right there by your side.'

'You were in the middle of your second-year exams. And they counted towards your degree.'

'That doesn't matter—I could always have resat them if I'd needed to. But *you* mattered, Alex. You did.' His voice was full of anguish, as if he were desperately try-ing to make her believe how much he'd cared about her.

'You weren't there,' she whispered. 'My whole world blew apart, and you weren't there. I was so desperate, I asked my parents to contact you—and you didn't come.'

'Your dad didn't ring me. I had no idea that any of this happened, Alex. You have to believe me.' He stroked her hair back from her forehead. 'I'm so sorry you had to go through that without my support. And yes, I would've walked out of my exams to be with you. Everything else would've sorted itself out later.'

'You didn't even send me a message. A card.'

'Because I didn't know what was going on. Anyway, I wouldn't have sent you a card. I would've been with you. End of.'

The worst thing was, she believed him.

She'd got him so badly wrong—just as he'd got her badly wrong. They'd both been too young to trust each other completely. And they'd lost half a lifetime together because of it.

'You were just eighteen, and you had to go through all that alone. That's awful.' He raked a hand through his hair. 'And I can understand now why you acted the way you did. You'd just found out you were expecting our baby—some-thing that was going to change your whole life, maybe turn all your plans upside down. And you rang me, only to get some strange woman who told you a pack of lies at a time when you were vulnerable enough not to question them. If you hadn't been scared and pregnant—not to mention full of hormones—you wouldn't have believed a word she'd said. You would've called me back later and demanded to know what the hell was going on.'

'And nobody told *you* the full truth, either.' She swallowed hard. 'I'm still furious that you thought I could ever—' she couldn't quite bring herself to say the words again '—do something like that, but I think now I can understand why you came to that conclusion.'

'That, and then Meggie telling me that you'd got married. Only a short time after you'd been pregnant with my baby.' He looked straight at her. 'What was I supposed to think? Obviously I wasn't that important to you, if you could marry someone else so fast.'

Nathan. The biggest mistake of her life. 'It wasn't quite like that.' She sighed. 'Let's just leave it that I was a bit mixed up at the time.'

'A bit?' he asked, sounding bitter.

'My life had changed completely. I was living in a damp little bedsit and working ridiculous hours to earn enough to support myself. I'd lost the man I loved, I'd lost our baby, and when someone sweeps you off your feet and makes you feel special and offers to take all the worries away...' She grimaced. 'I don't want to talk about my marriage.' She didn't even want to think about how bad her judgement had been. How much of herself she'd lost over those three years. 'Let's just leave it that it didn't work out.'

'For what it's worth,' he said gently, 'I'm truly sorry.'

His apology disarmed her. And he wasn't the only one at fault. She needed to take her share of the blame in what had happened. 'Me, too.'

'What you said about your Fallopian tube—did the doctors manage to fix it?' he asked.

She shook her head.

'So what does that mean for you?'

She'd known he'd ask that. Typical Jordan: she'd seen him in meetings and he always cut straight to the heart of the problem. She took a deep breath. 'If one of the tubes goes, it means that getting pregnant will be harder. And you have a slightly bigger risk than average of having another ectopic pregnancy next time round.'

'Is that why your marriage broke up?' he asked softly.

'Partly.' She swallowed hard. 'Please, can we just leave this now? I want to go home.'

Some of the pain in her voice must have touched him, because he nodded. 'I'll drive you.'

'A taxi's fine. If you don't mind me waiting here until it turns up.'

'In the circumstances, I think driving you home is the least I can do,' Jordan said. 'And yes, I know you're an adult and you're perfectly capable of ordering your own taxi. But right now I'm feeling bad about the way I believed the worst of you for all those years.' He looked awkward. 'I guess I'm better when I'm doing something practical.'

She could understand that. It was like that for her, too. That was one of the reasons why she was so hands-on in her job. 'Just as long as you don't expect to be offered coffee the other end,' she warned. 'Not because I still hate you, but because right now I'm all talked out and I can't handle any more tonight.'

'Understood. Shall we go?'

When she stood up, he moved to put his arms round her; she took a swift sidestep.

Pain flickered across his face. 'That wasn't a come-on, Alex. What you've just told me must've brought back

a lot, and it couldn't have been easy for you. I thought…'
He looked hurt. 'I just thought you could do with a hug.'

Yes. She wanted to be held. But then she knew she'd
start crying and make a fool of herself. There would be no
crying until she was back in her own flat, with a locked
door between her and the outside world. Nobody saw her
vulnerabilities, nowadays. *Nobody.* 'I'm fine.' But she stole
a glance at him and felt guilty; he looked drawn and miserable.

They went to his car in silence; but this time the atmo-
sphere was resigned rather than tense. Life had made them
both jaded and wary, she thought. And the way she'd dis-
appeared and then married someone else so quickly had
definitely played a part in making Jordan the way he was
now. The man she remembered had been full of laughter, enjoying clever jokes and wordplay. The man he was
now…She'd seen him smile, but he'd become so serious.
A workaholic.

Though who was she to judge? She knew that she was
just as bad.

'I'd better give you directions,' she said.

'No need.' He tapped her postcode into his satnav.

'How come you know my postcode?' she asked.

He shrugged. 'Your address was on your CV. I only
need to read things once to remember the salient points.'

Of course. He'd always been bright.

When they reached her flat, he insisted on seeing her
to her door. 'This isn't a bid for coffee. It's simply good
manners,' he said.

She didn't argue. But she nearly cracked when he said
gently, 'Are you going to be OK? Do you want me to call
Meggie for you?'

'I'll be fine,' she fibbed. 'But thanks for asking.'

'OK. I'll see you tomorrow.'

'Yeah. Thanks for the lift.'

'Pleasure.'

She closed the front door behind her, then leaned against the wall and sank down to the floor, wrapping her arms round her legs and resting her head against her knees. If things had only been different...

But they weren't.

And she and Jordan just had to put everything behind them, forget about tonight's revelations, and learn to work together.

CHAPTER FIVE

THE next day, Alexandra was in the office early. Though not early enough to avoid Jordan; when she walked into the staff kitchen, he was already there.

He looked at her, then took down another mug and spooned coffee into it. 'Morning. How are you doing?'

'Fine,' she lied. She noticed that he had dark smudges underneath his eyes; it looked as if he'd spent as bad a night as she had last night. 'Are you OK?' she asked.

He gave her a weary smile. 'I'm in meetings all day today. But text me if you need me, OK?'

Which didn't answer her question; and right now she didn't want to push. She didn't want to hear him say that he felt as bad as she did—and know that she was the cause of it.

'Coffee.' He pushed the mug along the worktop towards her.

'Thanks. I'll see you later. Enjoy your meetings.'

She didn't text him. Even though she was tempted. Going through everything again last night had stirred up all kinds of things—most of them unwelcome. Not just the memories of the pain she'd gone through, but things that she could barely admit to herself. Like the fact that she still found Jordan Smith attractive. Not just physically: she

liked the man he'd become. Straight-talking, yet responsible and thoughtful.

Which was another reason why she ought to avoid him.
She couldn't afford to let herself fall for him again. She'd
fought so hard for her independence and she didn't want to
lose a single iota of it. Jordan was used to being in charge,
and she'd had her fill of controlling men.

But the idea wouldn't go away, and her face grew hot
when he walked into her office at the end of the day.

'Had a good day?' he asked.

'Fine. You?'

'Fine.' He paused. 'You didn't text me.'

She shrugged. 'I didn't need to. I'm perfectly capable
of doing my job.'

'I know. Otherwise I wouldn't have hired you.' His gaze
held hers. 'And I didn't mean about work.'

Yeah. She knew that. She sighed. 'Jordan, what's past
is past. We can't change it. Only accept it.'

'Even though it makes me feel like pond life?'

She smiled. 'I don't see any signs of gills. Or slime.'

He inclined his head. 'Thank you for that. I wasn't fishing.'

'Well, no. If you're pond life, you'd be the one being
fished for.'

He smiled, then, and she wished she'd kept her mouth
shut. Because his smile was genuine, causing little crinkles
at the corners of his eyes. Crinkles she wanted to smooth
away with the tips of her fingers, before…

The blood rushed to her face as she realised what she
was thinking about. *Kissing Jordan.*

Interesting. She'd just gone really, really red. What was
she thinking about? Jordan wondered. But if he asked her
he knew she would back off rapidly. She was incredibly

wary of him; though that was hardly surprising, given what had happened to her. In her shoes, he'd be the same.

To make it easier for both of them, he brought the conversation back to business. 'How's the staff suggestion scheme going?'

'Good. I've had some really great ideas through it already,' she said.

'And I hear that every one of them has been acknowledged with a personal note, along with a chocolate Neapolitan that says "thank you" on the wrapper.'

She frowned. 'Is that a problem?'

'No. I was just wondering how big the chocolate bill is going to be.'

'It's not a marketing department expense. I bought them myself.'

Now that he hadn't expected. 'Why?'

'Because I want people to feel that they're appreciated— it's a small gesture, unexpected enough to please people but not expensive enough to embarrass them. And almost everyone likes chocolate.'

Yeah. He could remember lying in the park under the trees with his head in her lap, with her feeding him squares of chocolate. He could almost smell her light, floral scent, taste the sweetness of the chocolate, feel the silkiness of her hair against his face as she dipped her head to kiss him...

'Not expensive?' he said, trying to keep his thoughts on business instead of remembering what it was like to kiss the woman who sat at her desk, all cool and professional.

'I have a friend who produces promotional chocolates. If you choose a stock wrapper, like the one I use, you can buy them in reasonable quantities at less than the cost of, say, a small box of chocolates from Field's deli.'

'Define reasonable.'

'A box of fifty—so there isn't a storage problem like there would be if you had to buy a couple of thousand at a time.'

'Where do you store them?' he asked, curious.

She smiled. 'That's classified information, given how many chocoholics work on our floor.'

Including him. He fought to push the memories back. 'You've certainly made a hit.'

'And that's what I want Field's to do with our customers. Make them feel they're appreciated.'

He raised an eyebrow. 'You're going to send them chocolate, too?'

'No. I was thinking more along the lines of a points system. The more they interact on the website, the more points they get—and when they reach a certain level they'll get a store voucher.'

'Which we send out?'

'No. We give them a code they can use either online or at a till point in the store. And it's a unique code so it doesn't leave us open to fraud.'

She'd clearly thought this through properly, and he was impressed. And she'd follow it through, too, with her enthusiasm; he knew she'd carry the board of directors with her when she explained it to them.

Though all he could think of was how beautiful her mouth was as she spoke. And how that mouth had felt against his skin. And how the last time he'd really been happy was ten years ago, before they'd broken up.

Crazy. It couldn't work between them. No way would she let him close after what had happened. And he wasn't looking for a relationship in any case. He'd learned that lesson the hard way: they didn't work if you went in with your heart, and they didn't work if you went in with your head. Besides, he had enough on his plate with a department store to drag into this century.

Though he was having a seriously hard time getting Alexandra out of his head.

It got harder still during the rest of the week. She wasn't avoiding him, exactly—she was busy with events, and he had a week full of meetings—but when he did see her he realised that he liked the woman she'd become: bright, sparky, enthusiastic. She was good at her job; she came to him with solutions, not problems; and her ideas were creating a real buzz among customers and staff alike. Footfall in the store was up, and so were sales. Hiring her had definitely been the right thing for Field's; and he needed to keep his own feelings in the background.

On Friday evening, he dropped in to her office. 'Are you busy on Sunday?'

'Why?' she asked, looking wary.

'I was planning to go for a walk by the river in Greenwich. I wondered if you'd like to join me.'

'Is that a good idea?' she asked, looking warier still.

'Probably not,' he said. 'But I thought it might be nice to go for a walk and have an ice cream.'

She licked her lower lip, and a surge of longing filled him.

'That's a really bad idea,' she said, as if she'd guessed at his thoughts.

'OK.' He shrugged. 'Forget I asked.'

'I didn't say no,' she pointed out. 'Just that it's a bad idea.'

'So was that a roundabout way of saying yes?'

'A walk by the river and an ice cream,' she repeated.

Which was his version of an olive branch. 'Or a coffee if it turns out to be wet and freezing.'

'Wet and freezing works fine for me, where ice cream is concerned. What time?'

'Two? Three?'

'Two. Meet you outside the gates to the Royal Naval College—the ones nearest the Tube,' she said.

Funny how her agreement warmed him.

He was almost late. She was leaning against the iron railings, and she tapped her watch as he hurried to meet her. 'Tut. You're cutting it a bit fine, Mr Smith.'

'Blame the siren song of the spreadsheet,' he said, and she laughed.

She looked utterly gorgeous. Instead of the sharp business suits and high heels he was used to seeing her in, she was wearing faded denims, low-heeled boots and a bright red cashmere sweater beneath her open jacket. It made her look softer, younger—*touchable*. To the point where he had to jam his hands into the pockets of his own jeans to stop himself acting on the urge to pull her into his arms.

This was crazy. He shouldn't want to hold her, touch her, kiss her until they were both dizzy. But seeing her like this made the old desires flood all the way back.

They headed for the path by the river and walked together in silence for a while. Not an awkward silence, to his relief; more as if they were both wondering where this was going. As if they were both weighing up all the options.

'I've always liked this bit of London,' she said. 'Those gorgeous buildings. The domes.' She smiled. 'I always thought Rome would be like that.'

He remembered Italy being top of her travel wish-list when she was a teenager. Rome, Venice, Capri, Florence,

Pompeii, Vesuvius, Juliet's balcony in Verona: she'd wanted to see all of them. 'Did you ever get to see Rome?'

'Last year. A long weekend in Rome, seeing the Colosseum and the Pantheon and the Trevi Fountain. And the Sistine Chapel. It's the most beautiful city.'

'Yes, it is.' He found himself wondering who she'd gone with.

As if she'd guessed his thoughts, she said, 'Meggie told me I was crazy, going on my own. But I loved it—it meant I could see the places I wanted to see on *my* schedule, nobody else's.'

'There's nothing worse than having to rush round something you want to see because someone else thinks museums are boring,' he agreed.

She raised an eyebrow. 'That sounds personal. Did your wife—?' She broke off. 'Sorry. That was intrusive.'

'No, it's fine. She wasn't into museums. But she did like shopping, so we compromised in Rome. She enjoyed herself in the Via Condotti with my credit card, and I had the afternoon in the Capitoline Museum, among the sculptures.' He looked at her. 'Was your husband not keen on museums, either?'

'No,' she said, her voice crisp.

'Sorry. I didn't mean to pry.'

'It's OK.'

But he knew it wasn't; the wariness was back. Her marriage clearly hadn't been happy, or she wouldn't be divorced now. Or, he suddenly wondered, had she wanted to stay married but her ex had been the one to end it?

Not that he could ask her. She'd find it way too intrusive, and pushing would make her back off even more. And he didn't want her to back off. He wanted to get to know her again.

'So do you come here often?' she asked.

'Usually when I'm a bit out of sorts,' he said. 'I guess it's the flow of the water that makes me feel calmer.' He gave her a wry smile. 'And it's quicker to get to the Thames than it is to drive to the nearest beach.'

'I haven't been to the beach in years.'

She sounded wistful, and Jordan had the craziest idea. They'd managed a couple of days out to Brighton, that summer. OK, so you couldn't repeat the past. But you could still enjoy things second time round. Maybe he could take her to the beach for the day and it would bring a real smile back to her eyes.

He found a kiosk and bought them both an ice cream, then tempted her to take a taste of his. As their eyes met he remembered the times they'd done this in the past; he was pretty sure she was thinking of it, too. About how he'd lean forward and lick the smear of ice cream from the corner of her mouth. And then she'd turn her head very slightly towards him, lips parted, so his mouth could glide over hers. He'd nibble her lower lip until she sighed and slid her hands into his hair, letting him deepen the kiss.

He saw her eyes widen. Was she as close as he was to repeating it? What would she do if he leaned forward and kissed her? Probably run a mile, he acknowledged wryly. Now wasn't the right time. He'd know when that was— when they were both ready.

He kept the conversation neutral as they strolled along beside the Thames, and finally saw her home.

'Thank you. I've had a lovely time,' she said outside her front door.

'Me, too.'

She gave him a wry smile. 'Maybe I'll invite you in, next time.'

His heart skipped a beat. So there was going to be a next time. She felt it, too—and it wasn't just the past. It was who they were now. 'Sounds good,' he said, keeping his tone as light as possible.

He knew this was his cue to say goodbye. But he wasn't ready to leave her, not yet. Unable to help himself, he cupped her cheek.

Her eyes widened. 'Jordan.' Her voice was slightly deeper and huskier. Just as his would be, if he said her name. Almost rusty with desire.

His thumb was so close to her lower lip. All he had to do was move his hand. Very, very slightly stroke the pad of his thumb over her lower lip. Lightly, gently…

Risky. It might make her bolt.

On the other hand…

It was too much for him to resist. Barely making contact with her skin, yet feeling as if every nerve end were sizzling, he brushed the pad of his thumb over her lower lip.

Her pupils dilated even more, and her lips parted. He could feel the warmth of her breath against his skin, and it made his head spin. 'Alex,' he whispered, and dipped his head to kiss her. Sweet, soft, asking rather than demanding.

She kissed him back—tiny, nibbling kisses that heated his blood even more. But when his hands slid under her coat, drawing her closer to him, she pulled away.

'We shouldn't be doing this.'

He was about to tell her that she'd known damn well this would happen, when he noticed the panic in her eyes. No. It was going to happen. Both of them knew it. He just needed to give her a little more time to get used to the idea.

'I'd better go.' Even though he didn't want to. Every fibre of his being was begging him to stay. 'I'll see you later.'

The panic in her eyes started to ebb, and he knew he'd

made the right decision. And he also knew that she was
going to be worth waiting for.

From that point, it felt as if they'd reached a truce, and it
was a lot easier to work together. Jordan didn't feel as if
he had to watch what he said all the time, and she didn't
seem quite so reserved with him. Keeping his libido under
control was harder, though, and it didn't do his temper
much good.

In the middle of the week, Alexandra came into Jordan's
office. 'Can I run something past you?'

'What, now?'

She raised an eyebrow. 'Sorry. Is this a bad time?'

He sighed. 'No. Sorry. I shouldn't take my bad mood
out on you.'

'Problems?'

'No.'

'It sounds as if you need carbs.'

He frowned. 'What?'

'When did you last eat? A sandwich at your desk, was
it?'

'Don't make a big deal out of it. You do exactly the
same,' he said.

'True,' she admitted with a smile. 'OK. I'll leave you
to your bad mood.'

Except she didn't. Fifteen minutes later, she walked in
with a box of something that smelled delectable.

'Pizza?' he guessed.

'Yes. I went to that trattoria.'

'But they don't do takeaway food.'

'They do for you. I told Giorgio we were having a late
meeting and couldn't leave the computer. He says this is
your usual. *Funghi e prosciutto*.'

He really, really hadn't expected her to do that, and it threw him. 'I…Thank you, Alex.'

'*Prego.*' There was a hint of a teasing smile. 'As Giorgio would say.'

He wasn't surprised that she'd charmed the trattoria owner. She'd certainly charmed him. And he desperately wanted her to stay here a little longer. 'I hope you'll share it with me.'

'I…' She gave him a wary look.

'I don't bite,' he said softly. 'I know I growled at you earlier, and I apologise. I'm just out of sorts. And you're probably right, my blood sugar's a bit low.'

As they shared the pizza, once, his fingers brushed against hers, and it felt as if he'd been galvanised. He just hoped it hadn't shown on his face, because he didn't want her to bolt.

Then again, she could've made some excuse not to stay, not to share the pizza with him.

He looked at her hands. Beautiful hands, and such delicate fingers. She'd been able to bring him to his knees with her touch. He noticed a smear of tomato sauce on her thumb, and it was too much to resist. He picked up her hand and drew it to his mouth, licking the sauce away.

She dragged in a breath, and her eyes had gone wide.

Unable to stop himself, he drew the tip of her thumb into his mouth and sucked.

Oh, dear God. If Alexandra hadn't been sitting down, she would've fallen. Jordan had always been able to make her tremble with that beautiful, clever mouth. Pictures bloomed in her head; she could see herself sweeping everything off his desk. Pushing him across it. Straddling him…

She was practically hyperventilating now.

'Jordan. This is a bad idea.' She did her best to drag her

common sense from where it was hiding. 'I...this wasn't meant to be a seduction.'

'No. But it could be.' He moistened his lower lip with the tip of his tongue, making her wish it were her skin he was moistening. 'Alex.' His voice was low and sexy—and it made her wet when he said her name like that.

Oh, God. She was seconds away from losing her self control. From losing her mind, He'd stopped sucking her thumb, but his fingers were caressing her wrist, feeling the pulse thudding here.

She tried again. 'The pizza—I was just being nice. Doing what I'd do for any colleague.'

Liar. He didn't actually say it, but then again he didn't need to. They both knew.

But the panic must have shown in her face, because he released her hand. 'Thank you.' He paused and held her gaze. 'Lindsey certainly wouldn't have done that.'

'Lindsey being the former Mrs Smith?'

He sighed. 'Yes.'

She bit her lip. 'Sorry. I didn't mean to drag things up.'

'No, it's OK. The divorce was three years ago now. I'm fine.'

'Are you?'

'Actually, yes.' He grimaced. 'In hindsight, I shouldn't have married her. But at the time I thought I was doing the right thing. Dad was having chest pains, and I knew he was worrying about me settling down and being ready to take over from him.'

'Is your father OK now?'

'He's absolutely fine and enjoying retirement,' Jordan reassured her.

'That's good.' She paused. 'So you got married to keep your parents happy?'

'Not happy, exactly. But I knew they wanted to be sure

that I was settled.' He shrugged. 'I'd known Lindsey for years. She'd gone to the girls' school next door and we were friends.'

Given how badly things had gone wrong with Alexandra, Jordan had decided to choose his bride with his head rather than his heart. When he'd kissed Lindsey, his head hadn't filled with fireworks, the way it had when he'd kissed Alexandra, but he'd told himself that that was a good thing. He'd learned from Alexandra that love didn't stop you getting hurt, and so he'd chosen his wife *sensibly*. Someone from the same background as his own; someone who wanted the lifestyle he could give her and would be a corporate wife for him. 'I thought that our marriage would work out just fine.'

'But it didn't,' she said softly.

'No.' He sighed. 'It was my fault. I worked too many hours, didn't pay her enough attention, and she got bored waiting for me. She found someone else who was willing to give her what she needed, and she's much happier now.'

'Hard for you, though.'

Not as hard as it had been, losing Alexandra. Because, if he was honest about it, he'd never really loved Lindsey. Love hadn't been on his agenda. He'd thought that his head would steer him in the right direction, unlike the way his heart had steered him with Alexandra. And he'd still got it wrong. Ended up being hurt. Admittedly, his pride had been bruised slightly more than his heart, but it had still been a miserable time in his life. Since then, he'd kept all his relationships short and sweet. Non-existent, for the last six months, because he'd been concentrating on work.

'It wasn't great at the time, but I got over it.' He shrugged. 'As I said, I'm fine now.'

'Bored waiting for you.' Alexandra made a face. 'Didn't

she have a job, or at least do some charity work to stop herself being bored?'

'No.'

Alexandra's expression was unreadable. 'So she was a full-time WAG. Looked after financially by you, and her day was her own.'

He raised his eyebrows. 'Are you telling me you disapprove of WAGs?'

'Not all women like being looked after and told what to do.'

'I didn't tell Lindsey what to do,' he said dryly. 'But isn't that meant to be the dream? Not having to drag yourself out of bed every Monday morning and know you're going to spend the week having to deal with office politics or difficult customers, not to mention worrying about whether the company's going to go under and you'll still have a job at the end of the week?'

She thought about it. 'Maybe for a couple of days it'd be nice not to have any worries or responsibilities. But the idea of every single day being the same—a session with a personal trainer, then off to be pampered at the beauty parlour, then lunch with the girls, then mooching around the shops, then waiting for my husband to come home so I could tell him all about my, oh, so exciting day...' She shook her head. 'I'd be bored to tears within a week. Not to mention the fact I'd rather earn my own money and not have to be accountable to someone else for every penny I spent.'

That sounded a bit heartfelt. 'Are you talking from experience?' he asked.

For a moment, he thought she was going to back away, but then she gave him a sad little smile. 'Yes.'

She'd said that her marriage hadn't worked out. Clearly she'd been unhappy with Bennett. But Jordan didn't understand why she'd had to account to her husband for every penny she'd spent, when she'd been earning. There'd been no gaps in her CV. She'd always had a job.

'Jordan,' she warned, 'your thoughts are written all over your face. Don't ask.'

'OK.' Clearly it was too painful for her to talk about. 'For what it's worth,' he said, 'I'm sorry your marriage didn't work out. I was hurt and angry when I found out you'd got married to someone else so soon after me, and I hated you for a while—but I wouldn't have wished you anything else but happiness.' Her eyes were suspiciously shiny, and he saw her blink back a tear. 'And I'm sorry. I didn't mean to rip open any scars just now.'

'Not your fault.' She took a deep breath. 'I rushed into getting married. I thought Nathan would give me everything you and my parents hadn't. What you said about being looked after—that's what I wanted, back then.' She bit her lip. 'Except it didn't turn out quite how I thought it would.'

Accountable for every penny she spent. Clearly the man had taken 'looking after' to the extreme. Jordan had never expected Lindsey to tell him what she'd bought; he'd simply picked up the bills, thinking that as long as she was happy everything would be fine.

He reached across his desk and squeezed Alexandra's hand. He kept holding it for just long enough to let her know that he was on her side, then withdrew his hand again so she'd know he wasn't going to crowd her. Wasn't going to push her, the way he had when he'd drawn her thumb into his mouth. 'It's easy to be wise with hindsight,' he said. 'But you just have to do the best you can, based on the knowledge you have at that moment.'

'I guess so.'

'Sometimes you have to stop beating yourself up about

things you would've done differently.' He gave her a rueful smile. 'And that's easier said than done. I'm still find-
ing it hard to forgive myself now I know what happened
to you.'

He didn't know the half of it, Alexandra thought. And she
wasn't ready to tell him the rest of it. About how she'd
struggled to support herself. How she'd been so ready to
fall for Nathan's promise of a happy-ever-after. And how,
when she hadn't been able to hold up her side of the bar-
gain, Nathan had never let her forget how she'd failed him.
She'd failed to give him the family he wanted, failed to
suppress her own needs and make him the centre of her
world instead of dreaming about finally taking her degree,
failed to be the dutiful and biddable wife he'd expected.

'It wasn't all your fault. I made some bad choices, too.'
She lifted her chin. 'And we're both in danger of getting really maudlin. So I'm going home.' She paused long enough
to make it clear that it wasn't an offer for him to join her.
'And I hope you're not intending to stay at your desk until
midnight.'

'Not quite. Though there was something I wanted to
finish tonight,' Jordan said.

'Don't work too late.' She took the pizza box with her,
and disposed of it in the bin in the staff kitchen, then
headed back to her own office, backed up her files and
switched off the computer. And then, on impulse, she took
something from her filing cabinet, placed it in a small
envelope from her recycling tray, and walked back into
Jordan's office.

'See you tomorrow,' she said.

'See you tomorrow,' he echoed. 'And thank you for the
pizza.'

'Pleasure. Oh, by the way, I have something for you.'
She handed him the envelope.

'What's this?'

She simply smiled. 'Open it later.'

When she'd gone, Jordan opened the envelope. It contained
one of the infamous chocolate Neapolitans she sent out
with her acknowledgement notes for the staff suggestion
scheme. *Thank you.* What was she thanking him for? he
wondered. For listening to her tonight, or for not pushing
her to go to bed with him, or for not pushing her to tell him
everything about her unhappy marriage? Clearly whatever
had gone wrong had left deep scars—and he didn't have a
magic wand to whisk them away. If he'd taken proper care
of her in the first place, she wouldn't have ended up marrying the guy, so he definitely had a share in the blame.

Where did they go from here? He really didn't know.
But she'd given him an opening with the chocolate, and
he intended to make the most of it.

CHAPTER SIX

THE brown envelope on Alexandra's desk contained a small box and a sticky note that said, *Chocolate: raise you one.*

Jordan hadn't signed the note; then again, he hadn't needed to. His handwriting was bold and confident, like the man himself.

She opened the envelope to discover a small box containing a single gold-foiled chocolate. So he was claiming this was better than her Neapolitans, was he? As if. She smiled, and left it in the box until her mid-morning coffee.

The chocolate melted in her mouth; she'd never, ever tasted anything so good. She could brazen it out and pretend that she thought it was perfectly ordinary, but that way she wouldn't find out what it was and where she could get more. And she had to push away the sudden vision of him feeding her the chocolates one by one—in bed.

She emailed him.

You win. Stockist details required, pls.

The reply came back swiftly.

Field's deli. Tut. I expect my marketing manager to be a *bit* more observant.

Though there wasn't an edge to his tone. She could imagine him laughing as he wrote the email. And she liked this fun, teasing side of him. More than liked. If she wasn't careful, she could find herself falling for him again. Not that she'd act on it, this time round. Her life was back on track, and she intended to keep it that way. Yes, she could go to bed with him; and yes, it would be good for both of them. But she couldn't trust herself to keep it just physical—and no way did she want to risk her heart again.

The wonderful chocolate turned out to be Italian. So how did she top that? She went for a walk during her lunch break, still thinking about it, and found a tiny market stall that sold handmade chocolate by a local chocolatier. Chocolate that, according to the notices on the stall, had won awards. A quick chat with the chocolatier netted her something that she was confident might just raise the stakes. Back at the store, she discovered that Jordan was in a meeting, so she left him an envelope containing a dark chocolate praline and a white chocolate square scented with lavender, plus a sticky note saying, *Raise you two.*

She'd just finished double-checking a set of figures for a report when her computer pinged to tell her that an email had arrived.

This isn't ours. Why not?

She typed back.

Clarification required. Why not = why use a competitor, or = when can we make them a stockist?

Jordan didn't waste words.

Both. Can you get samples and contact details to Sally? Thanks.

Sally was the deli manager, a real foodie who loved her job; and Alexandra had thoroughly enjoyed talking to her about her idea for developing specialist hampers—particularly as sampling had been involved.

Sure.

The chocolate—and the talk they'd had over takeaway pizza at his desk—had gone a long way to thawing out their relationship; not just the business side of things, showing them that they could work together for the good of Field's, but personally, too. A couple of times, Jordan talked her into going to the trattoria with him; although they spent most of their time talking shop, more personal stuff had started creeping in.

It really didn't help that she found him so attractive still. Why couldn't he have turned into a short, overweight, middle-aged businessman with greasy hair, terrible skin and bad teeth? Then she might not have found herself thinking about him so much...

There was a rap on her door, and she looked up from her desk to see the subject of her thoughts standing there. 'Got a second?'

'Sure.'

He walked into her office and sat down on the chair next to her desk. 'Are you busy tomorrow evening?'

'No.'

'Then I wondered if you might come somewhere with me.'

Work, she presumed. 'You're going to see a new supplier? Sure.'

'Not a new supplier.' He took his mobile phone from his pocket, flicked into the Internet, and passed the phone to her. His fingers brushed against hers as she took the phone, and every nerve ending in her skin tingled.

She stared at the screen, really hoping that she wasn't blushing, because her face felt incredibly hot. *'Antony and Cleopatra.'* A seriously good production, too. It had been one of her A level set texts and she'd loved the play. Was this simply a coincidence, or did he remember? 'You've got tickets for this?'

He nodded. 'I was going with a friend, but she can't make it now.'

A friend. A *female* friend. His girlfriend? No, of course not. She knew now that he wasn't the kind of man who'd cheat. But she still couldn't help the question. 'Will your girlfriend mind you taking me?'

'Siobhan's not my girlfriend. Just a friend.'

'I see.'

'She's married to my best friend,' he explained. 'And the reason she's not coming is because she has morning sickness that seems to last all day. Our tickets are in the middle of the row and she's terrified she won't be able to escape to the loo in time if she starts feeling ill.'

'I see,' Alexandra said again. Her heart contracted sharply at the mention of morning sickness. It wasn't something she'd ever suffered; both times she'd been pregnant, things had gone wrong well before she'd reached that stage. Then she realised that Jordan was waiting for her to say something. She tamped down her feelings and tried to sound sympathetic. 'Poor woman.'

'She's really disappointed about missing this. Hugo loathes Shakespeare—which is probably Siobhan's fault for taking him to see a really avant-garde version of one of the minor plays, years ago, instead of breaking him in gently—so the deal is that I go with her to any Shakespeare she wants to see and he goes to all the comedies and lighter dramas with her.'

His best friend's wife. *Really* just a friend, then. Though she didn't quite understand why Jordan was still single. The man she was getting to know was the man she'd wished he'd been, ten years before.

'So would you like to go with me?' he asked.

'Yes, please. As long as I can pay for my own ticket.'

He sighed. 'That's not necessary. I've had the tickets for months, so they would've been wasted if you'd said no—and actually it'll be nice to share it with someone who knows the play as well as you do.'

So he *did* remember that it was one of the texts she'd studied.

'I'll pick you up at seven,' he said.

Too close to Nathan, organising her and always being in charge. She'd rather make her own way there. 'How about I meet you in the foyer at seven?'

'If that's what you'd prefer.'

'Thank you. Seven it is, then.'

Alexandra found it hard to concentrate on work for the whole of Friday, and she agonised all the way home about what to wear. She knew that people didn't dress up so much for the theatre nowadays, but even so jeans would feel wrong. In the end, she decided on a little black dress, the designer shoes that always made her feel confident, and minimum make-up and jewellery; that way, she wouldn't be so dressed up that she'd draw attention to herself, but she wouldn't be too casual, either.

Jordan was already waiting for her in the foyer; like her, he was dressed smart-casual, in dark trousers and a cashmere sweater that brought out the blue in his eyes. Alexandra's heart skipped a beat as he raised a hand to acknowledge her and walked to meet her, smiling.

Oh, help. She really had to remember that this wasn't a date; it was simply a matter of not letting good tickets go to waste. Being practical.

'I'm glad you could make it.' For a moment, she thought he was going to kiss her cheek; then he clearly thought better of it and moved back just a fraction. Just as well, because she wasn't sure she could cope with the feel of his lips against her skin. She might do something truly stupid—like turning her head slightly so his mouth met hers, and…

'Can I get you a drink?' he asked.

'I'm fine, thanks.' And it was ridiculous to feel so nervous. They were colleagues. Maybe even starting to be friends.

'I took the liberty of getting you a programme. And don't you dare offer to reimburse me,' he added, 'because I would've done the same for Siobhan.'

'Thank you.' She'd accept his kindness. To a point. She still wasn't going to compromise her independence. 'And in return you can let me buy you a drink in the interval.'

'Sure. Shall we go and find our seats?'

He placed his hand under her elbow to guide her through the crush, and Alexandra instantly regretted wearing a sleeveless dress. The touch of his skin against hers sent desire licking all the way down her spine. A thick woollen sweater would've been much safer. Or maybe a full suit of armour.

The seats were close enough together that, when the row was full, Jordan's leg was forced against hers. The lick of desire grew stronger; at this rate, Alexandra thought, by the end of the evening she was going to be a complete puddle of hormones.

To her relief, the safety curtain finally went up and the play began. The cast was strong, and she was soon absorbed in the sheer poetry of the words.

On stage, Enobarbus waxed lyrical about the queen. 'The barge she sat in, like a burnish'd throne…'

Jordan's fingers curled round hers. Lost in the magic of the play, she didn't pull away; but when the curtain came down for the interval she realised that they were still holding hands, their fingers tightly linked.

Oh, help. This wasn't on the agenda for either of them.

'Um, shall we get a drink?' she asked brightly.

She could see in his eyes that he was tempted to call her on her refusal to mention the fact that they were holding hands. But then he disentangled his fingers from hers without comment. 'Sure.'

She bought them both a glass of wine; and she was aware that she was drinking hers much too fast. That, or Jordan's nearness was making her head spin. Where was a cold shower when you needed one?

To her relief, he didn't take her hand again when they returned to their seats. She lost herself in the play again, until the moment when Antony died and Cleopatra realised what she'd lost. 'There is nothing left remarkable Beneath the visiting moon.'

Alexandra remembered exactly how that felt. The bleakness of the days when she realised exactly what she'd lost—the love of her life, their baby, and her future. Days when nothing could touch her or drag her out of the pit of despair, not even the books she'd once loved so much. She hadn't taken them with her when she'd left home; she wondered if her parents had kept them for her in the attic.

Or maybe they'd taken them to the nearest charity shop, to get all the clutter out of the way.

She felt her eyes fill with tears; frantically, she tried to blink them back, but it didn't work. She dared not rub her eyes and draw Jordan's attention to the fact she was crying, in case he pushed to find out why—yes, the play was moving, but he was bright. He'd work out that there was more to it than that. He'd ask what was wrong. And he'd ask until he got a proper answer.

She blinked as hard as she could, but several tears escaped and slid silently down her cheeks.

Outside the theatre, he noticed immediately that her eyes were red. 'You were crying,' he said softly.

'Sorry, that play always moves me. Even though I think Cleopatra's a selfish, manipulative attention-seeker, she really did love Antony.' Just as she'd loved Jordan. With all her heart. Before he broke it into tiny pieces. 'It's been a very long time since I've seen it.' She drew in a shaky breath. 'Thank you so much for bringing me.'

'My pleasure.' He looked awkward. 'I'd better get us a taxi.'

He managed to hail one almost instantly. 'I'll drop you off first,' he said.

'Thank you.' She gave the taxi driver her address.

Jordan wasn't holding her hand in the taxi, but she could still feel the warmth and pressure of his fingers curled round hers. And, when the car pulled up outside her flat, she gave in to the mad impulse and said, 'Do you want to come in for a coffee?'

Jordan looked at her. 'Are you sure?'

No. This could turn out to be a huge mistake. 'I'm sure,' she fibbed.

'Then thank you.' And his smile made her knees feel as if they'd just melted.

'Make yourself at home,' she said as she unlocked the front door and ushered him into her flat. 'I'll bring the coffee through.'

Alexandra's flat was small, Jordan thought, much smaller than his own, and decorated in neutral tones. Her living room was only just big enough for a sofa, a TV, an audio system, and a single bookcase. There was a framed print of a Whistler nocturne on one wall, but the only photographs on the mantelpiece were of her with Meggie on what was obviously Meggie's wedding day, two more of her holding a baby—which he guessed were the godchildren she'd mentioned at the story-time session—and what were obviously the latest school photographs of the two children, one of eleven or twelve and one who looked about six. But there were none of Alexandra's parents, which struck him as odd; he remembered her being reasonably close to them, ten years ago.

She'd told him that things had been strained after she'd lost the baby, but clearly their relationship hadn't been repaired. Why? Because of her divorce? Had they approved of the man she'd married, or had he come between Alexandra and her family? He didn't have a clue, but he didn't want to scare her off by asking her. Not now she'd actually asked him into her flat, let him that little tiny bit closer.

There also weren't many books; that single bookcase also held a selection of music and films. Again, it surprised him; he could still remember the time when Alexandra's parents had been out and she'd sneaked him up to her room. There had been two huge bookcases in her bedroom, completely stuffed with books, as well as a big pile next to her desk. But there wasn't a single academic book on her shelves now. No poetry, no Shakespeare, no plays.

Most of them were marketing textbooks. And it just didn't feel right. Didn't feel like *her*.

He wandered into her equally tiny kitchen. There was barely enough space for both of them in the room. He could smell the vanilla base of her perfume, and it made him want to taste her. He'd promised himself he'd give her time, but his resistance crumbled like sand. 'Alex,' he said softly.

She turned round to face him, her eyes huge, and he was lost; he dipped his head and brushed his mouth against hers. Her lips were so soft; he couldn't resist doing it again and again, catching her lower lip between his and sucking. When her lips parted, he deepened the kiss, sliding one hand against her nape and the other at the base of her spine, drawing her closer to him.

Heaven.

It had been so long since he'd felt like this. Years.

Kissing Alexandra…

Oh, God. He wasn't supposed to be doing this. He broke the kiss and dropped his hands, though there wasn't enough room for him to take a proper step back from her. 'I'm sorry. That wasn't meant to happen.'

'No.' But she was staring at his mouth. She glanced up at him again, just like the first time he met her, and he couldn't resist. He needed to kiss her. Here. Now. Before he imploded. He bent his head again to kiss her, and this time she slid her arms round his neck and was kissing him back. It felt like coming home after too many years away, which was utterly crazy. What happened to keeping some professional distance between them? What happened to being just close enough to have a decent working relationship?

'Alex.' Her name was ripped from him.

'It's Xandra nowadays,' she reminded him.

He shook his head. 'You'll always be Alex to me.'

'I'm not the person I was back then,' she warned. 'I'm not looking for love any more. I'm older and wiser.'

'I know. Me, neither.' He stroked her cheek.

She swallowed hard. 'This thing between us. We can ignore it.'

'Of course we can. We're both intelligent adults.'

And he really, really needed to kiss her again. Preferably in the next nanosecond.

Things felt much, much better when her mouth was moving against his. She was kissing him back; her hands slid underneath his sweater, stroking his skin, and it felt so, so good. He loved the feeling of her skin against his, though he wanted more. He was burning up with need and desire.

Then she broke the kiss. 'Jordan. We can't do this.'

'No?' His head was swimming.

'It went wrong between us before. I don't want to complicate things at work.'

Work. He'd forgotten about that. Completely. How? Field's was the centre of his life; it had been for years. How had he completely blocked that out? He dragged in a breath. 'OK. You're right. We'll be sensible. We'll keep things strictly business between us. And I'd better not stay for coffee.' He couldn't trust himself not to kiss her again.

'Let me call you a taxi.'

'It's OK. I'll find one. I need some air.' To clear his head. Hell, if he had to walk back to his flat in Notting Hill, it wouldn't matter. And it probably still wouldn't be enough fresh air to wipe the memories from his head. 'I'll, um, see you at Field's.'

'Yeah.'

'I'll see myself out.'

* * *

Alexandra waited until he'd closed her front door behind her before she sank down on the kitchen floor, drew her knees up to her chin and wrapped her arms round her legs. The tears she'd tried to stem in the theatre slid down her cheeks, unchecked.

If only things could've been different.

Even though she knew now that he hadn't cheated on her—that she would've been able to rely on him—her marriage had corroded her ability to trust. She couldn't take the risk of a relationship with another man who was used to being in charge, a man who'd boss her around and tell her what to do. Maybe with the best of intentions, but he'd still tell her what to do.

And there was the other issue, too. Jordan had said nothing about whether he'd wanted a family with his wife—or in the future, for that matter—but she knew that he was the fourth generation of his family to head up the business. So it was more than likely that he'd want an heir—an heir she couldn't give him without an awful lot of medical intervention. Intervention she just hadn't been able to face, no matter how much Nathan had gone on and on and on about how she was being weak and feeble and pathetic and a coward. Maybe Jordan's reaction would be different; but she really didn't want to see the pity in his eyes when he knew the full story.

So she was just going to have to be strong. Resist everything her heart was telling her. Her heart had got things so wrong in the past; from now on, she was only listening to her head. And her head was definitely telling her the right thing. The sensible thing.

Stay away from Jordan Smith.

CHAPTER SEVEN

JORDAN found himself reading the same page of the financial report for the third time. And it still made no sense, because all he could think about was Alexandra. The way he'd kissed her. The way she'd responded. And the way she'd run scared.

He was the one who'd said it would be strictly business between them from now on.

What an idiot he was. How could it possibly be just business between them, when every day he worked with her was torture? Being in a meeting with her, when he was close enough to smell her scent or feel her fingers brush against his as she handed him a piece of paper...The last week had driven him crazy. He was aware that he'd been snapping at everyone; Alexandra, on the other hand, had managed to stay absolutely professional and treated him exactly the same way that she treated everyone else.

Except, despite what he'd said to her, that wasn't what he really wanted. And he'd caught her eye enough times, seen the wistfulness in her face that she hadn't been quite quick enough to mask, to think that it wasn't what she wanted, either.

It made no sense. Last time they'd been together, they'd crashed and burned. How could it possibly be any different, this time round?

Yet he wanted her. More than he'd wanted anyone in his entire life.

He glanced at his watch. Half-past seven. Everyone else on their floor would have gone home by now; the only people here were the security team. And Alexandra.

He backed up his files, turned off his computer, and went to her office, pausing in the doorway. She clearly hadn't heard him because she simply continued working; he could see how much she was concentrating, because she'd caught the tip of her tongue between her teeth.

Her mouth was driving him crazy.

Everything about her was driving him crazy.

And he needed to do something about it.

He knocked on the open door, and walked in as she looked up.

'Did you want something?' she asked.

Yes. He wanted her.

He sat on the edge of her desk. 'This isn't working.'

There was a flare of panic in her eyes. 'What isn't?'

'We have unfinished business, Alex, and you know it.'

'No.' She dragged in a breath. 'We agreed we'd keep it to just work between us.'

He shook his head. 'I don't think I can do that any more. I'm not sure you can, either.' He looked straight at her. 'And I don't want to talk about it here. Your place or mine?'

'Just to talk,' Alexandra said.

In answer, he spread his hands, as if to say, *What do you think?*

No, it wasn't going to be just talking. The two of them, alone, in a private space…it was obvious what was going to happen. What had been waiting to happen for days. What had been making her pulse race, every time she was in a meeting with him. What she couldn't get out of her head.

She licked her dry lower lip. 'Yours,' she whispered.

He picked up her phone and ordered a taxi; it was all she could do to keep her gaze off his hands. Beautiful hands. Hands that she so desperately wanted to touch her—even though she knew that this was the worst idea either of them had ever had.

As soon as she'd backed up her files and switched off the machine, he said, 'Let's go.'

The taxi was already waiting outside. Neither of them said a word on the way to Jordan's flat. He still wasn't talking when he ushered her into the lift. But she could practically feel the tension radiating off him; so he wasn't as cool and calm as he was trying to make out. Just as she was trying to preserve a façade of coolness and control, when inside she was shaking with need and anger and desire, all mixed up together.

He unlocked the front door and gestured for her to go inside. The second he'd closed the door behind them, he pulled her into his arms and jammed his mouth over hers. It wasn't a sweet, gentle, persuading kiss. It was an angry kiss, full of frustration and desire and need. A kiss that she matched, touch for touch and bite for bite.

When he lifted his head again, they were both shaking.

'This is insane. It shouldn't be happening.' He shook his head in seeming exasperation. 'I shouldn't want you this much.'

The confession undid her. 'Me, neither,' she whispered.

'Alex, I haven't slept properly in a week. All I can see is you. All I can feel is you. I even dream about you, for heaven's sake.'

She lifted her hand and laid her palm against his cheek. 'We said we'd keep it strictly business.'

'It's a hell of a lot easier said than done.' He looked tortured. 'I'm starting to think about opening a branch in

Australia and going there to set it up myself. Being half a world away from you might just help.' Though then he turned his face so his lips were against her palm. Pressed the softest, sweetest kiss against her skin. And it made her want to cry. Why were they both making this so complicated when it should be so simple?

'Opening a branch on the moon wouldn't help,' she said, her voice ragged. 'Or on Mars. Or even on the other side of the Milky Way. Because I'd still be thinking about you.'

Her admission made him crack. He cupped her face in his hands and brushed his mouth against hers in the sweetest, most cherishing kiss; then he bent to scoop one hand behind her knees, lifted her up and carried her down the corridor to his bedroom. When he set her back on her feet again, he made sure that her body was pressed against his all the way, leaving her in no doubt of just how much he wanted her.

She wanted him, too. Wanted to feel his hands on her body, his mouth on her skin. She wanted to touch him, too—so much that it made her ache for him.

He undid her shirt, taking it slowly, keeping his gaze fixed on hers. Once he'd pushed the soft cotton over her shoulders, he took a step back and just looked at her. And it was just like the very first time he'd done that, the weekend she'd turned eighteen. When he'd slowly undressed her, touched her, taught her body exactly how much pleasure he could give her.

Now, as then, the intensity of his gaze made her feel shy—and yet, at the same time, it made her feel hot. Thrilled that she could turn this gorgeous, clever man to mush, push everything out of his mind except her.

'You're beautiful, Alex.' The admission was almost ripped from him, and heat pooled in her stomach. He reached out, moulding her curves with his palms.

Back then, she'd been a girl. A shy virgin. When he'd stroked her to her very first climax, she'd been shocked by how he'd made her feel, as if the universe were splintering round her.

She wasn't a shy, naïve teenager any more. She knew what to expect. And although it had been years since they'd touched each other this intimately, she knew it was still going to be the same between them—that same flaring, intense heat.

'Jordan. I want you,' she whispered, and drew her tongue along her lower lip.

'Good,' he said.

He drew each shoulder strap of her bra down in turn before kissing his way along her exposed skin. So slowly that it was driving her mad; she wanted to be skin to skin with him. Here. Now. *Right now.*

'So soft. So smooth. So kissable.' He kissed his way along the edge of her bra. 'And here...' He nuzzled the peak of her nipple, and the friction of the lace against her sensitised skin made her gasp.

And then she stopped thinking at all as his mouth closed over her nipple. Hot. Wet.

'Jordan,' she whispered. 'Now.'

'I know.' His voice was husky as he straightened up again and looked her straight in the eye. 'I want you so much, it hurts. I want to be inside you right this very moment. But at the same time I want to take it slowly, savour every second of this.'

Fast and slow, all at the same time. She knew exactly what he meant: it was the same for her. She wanted everything, all at once.

The intense look of desire in his eyes gave her licence to do anything she pleased. She removed his tie, then undid the buttons of his shirt; she took her time, retaliating for the way he'd undressed her so slowly. The pads of her fingertips teased his skin, moving in tiny circles in a way that she knew would arouse him to fever pitch, the same way he'd aroused her.

He was shaking slightly, clearly trying to stay in control—and she needed him to lose it as much as she had. She let his shirt fall to the floor, then leaned forward and pressed a hot, open-mouthed kiss against his throat. He arched his head back, giving her better access, and closed his eyes in seeming bliss as she nibbled her way across his skin.

She took her time removing his trousers; finally, his control snapped, and he kissed her hard. The next thing she knew, they were both naked, she was in his arms, and he was lifting her onto the bed.

She reached up to trace his lower lip with a fingertip.

He moved to catch her finger between his lips, and sucked.

'Oh, my God, Jordan. That's…'

'Yeah. Me, too.' He kissed her throat, nuzzled the hollows of her collarbones; in turn she stroked him, touched him, urged him on.

He moved lower, took one nipple into his mouth and sucked. This time, there was no lace in the way: just his lips and his tongue and his teeth, teasing her and arousing her until her hands were fisted in his hair and her breathing was fast and shallow.

'I'm not finished with you yet. Not by a long way,' he whispered against her skin. He moved lower, nuzzling her belly, and slid one hand between her thighs.

Her pulse rate spiked. 'Please, Jordan.' When he skated a fingertip across her clitoris, she was completely lost. She tilted her hips, needing him deeper, harder.

He went still. 'We need a condom.'

No, we don't, she thought. The bitter irony wasn't lost on her. What broke them up in the first place couldn't happen at all now. She couldn't get pregnant just by making love. She couldn't make a baby—not without a huge amount of medical help and an even bigger bit of luck. It wasn't a real option for her any more.

But it hurt too much to say it. Her throat felt as if it was closing up.

'Alex—hold on.' Luckily for her, he misinterpreted what had made her freeze. He stroked her face, then climbed off the bed and rummaged in his pocket for his wallet. He gave a sigh of relief as he took out a foil packet, ripped it open, slid the condom on to protect her. Then at last, he eased inside her.

And it was heaven.

She wrapped her legs round his waist to draw him deeper. It had never been like this with anyone else. Only with Jordan had she felt this soul-deep connection.

'You feel amazing,' he whispered.

'So do you.' Her voice sounded shaky, even to herself. How long had it been since someone had said that to her— had made love to her just for herself, instead of trying for a baby?

He stopped moving and propped himself on his elbows so he could look her in the eye. 'OK?' he asked softly.

She nodded, not trusting herself to speak.

'If you want me to stop, I will.' He touched her cheek with the backs of his fingers. 'This isn't just about me. I want you with me all the way.'

She shook her head. 'This shouldn't be happening,' she whispered. 'We should stop this right now.' She dragged in a breath. 'Except I don't want you to stop.'

'I don't want to stop, either.' He lowered his mouth to hers in a warm, sweet, reassuring kiss.

Pleasure started to spiral through her; as if he knew, he slowed everything right down, focusing on the pleasure and stretching it out. She gasped as he pushed deeper, deeper. 'Jordan, *yes.*' And then she felt her body begin to tighten round his, pulse after pulse of sheer, mind-drugging pleasure.

'Alex,' he sighed, and she felt his body surge against hers.

He stayed where he was, just holding her close; finally, he eased out of her. 'I'll just deal with the condom.'

While he was in the bathroom, Alexandra's doubts flooded back. No way was she going to be able to stay naked in his bed. She retrieved her scattered clothing. Everything looked horribly crumpled, but the dry-cleaner would be able to sort out her suit later. She'd just finished buttoning her shirt when Jordan walked back in—completely naked. Not even a towel wrapped loosely round his hips.

'Right. So I'm at the disadvantage now,' he said dryly.

'Should I, um, turn my back while you get dressed?'

'Whatever,' he drawled.

'I, um…I'll just get myself a glass of water in the kitchen. If you don't mind.' She could feel her face turning crimson.

'Sure.'

She grabbed her shoes and fled; but the cold water did nothing to ease the heat in her face. Why the hell hadn't she had more self-control?

Jordan joined her in the kitchen, wearing dark trousers and the same cashmere sweater he'd worn to the theatre. The one that had made her want to touch him. Her fingers itched to stroke the soft material, but that would be a liberty too far. Especially as she knew that she wouldn't be able to stop at just touching the cashmere.

'OK. So this was a mistake. But it doesn't have to affect us at work,' she said. 'We just got a bit mixed up and forgot who and where we were. We'll just pretend on Monday morning that it never happened.'

'I'm not sure I can do that.'

She bit her lip. 'So what, then?'

'Neither of us can keep our hands off each other.' He looked at her. 'Every time I see you, I want to touch you, kiss you until we're both dizzy and carry you to my bed. And don't tell me it's not the same for you, Alex.'

She was about to protest that it wasn't, when he circled her hardened nipple with one fingertip. Heat burned through her face.

'Admit it. You want me as much as I want you.'

'Yes.' She couldn't lie. Not with the physical evidence so damn obvious to both of them. 'But I'm not looking for a relationship.'

'Neither am I.' He held her gaze. 'But I can't get you out of my head.'

'Maybe it's just a physical thing and it'll burn itself out.' She dragged in a shaky breath. 'Maybe we should…' The words stuck in her throat.

'Avoid each other?' He spread his hands. 'That's not an option. We can't avoid each other at work. And we need to talk about this, Alex. Ignoring it won't make it go away.'

She leaned her forehead against his. 'This whole thing scares the hell out of me.'

'If it helps, you're not the only one,' he said dryly. 'Here's an idea. I'll drive you home. You ring me tomorrow morning when you wake up. I'll bring breakfast over. And then we'll decide what we want to do for the rest of the day.'

She frowned. 'It's Saturday. Aren't you going to be at work?'

'I do take the occasional day off. And I happen to know you don't have any events on tomorrow, so you're not in work either. So, is it a deal?'

A whole day with Jordan. Doing anything they liked. Free just to be themselves, to be with each other. It was so very, very tempting…

'Is it a deal?' he repeated.

She nodded. 'Deal.'

'Let's go. And be clear about this, Alex—I'd rather you stayed here with me tonight. Much rather.' His gaze held hers. 'But I think you need a bit of space, and if that makes the difference between you running scared and you spending tomorrow with me, then I'll live with that.'

'Thank you,' she said softly.

He kissed her. 'Let's go. While I still have some control over myself.'

CHAPTER EIGHT

THE next morning, Alexandra rang Jordan at eight.

'You've only just woken up?' he asked, sounding surprised.

'No, I've been up for a couple of hours.' She'd barely slept; not that she was going to tell him that.

'So have I.' His voice softened. 'Why didn't you ring me earlier?'

'Because I didn't want to be too pushy,' she admitted.

He laughed. 'I nearly drove over at six without ringing you first. I wish I had, now. Still. I'll see you in twenty minutes with breakfast.'

Alexandra had already showered and dressed, and had been trying to distract herself with a mug of coffee and a cryptic crossword. Not that it had worked; she hadn't been able to stop thinking about him. Wanting him. 'See you in twenty minutes,' she said.

It gave her enough time to tidy the flat for the second time that morning, put the kettle on and lay the kitchen table for breakfast; but all the while butterflies were stampeding in her stomach. Today was the first real day of their fling. Would it turn out to be the best idea she'd ever had—or the very, very worst?

Jordan turned up dead on time, carrying two brown paper bags. 'I'm parked outside, completely illegally. Do you have a visitor permit, or is there a non-resident parking zone somewhere nearby?'

'I've got a visitor permit,' she said 'You just need to fill in the time and your registration number.'

He followed her into the kitchen; she took a visitor permit from the drawer where she kept them and handed it to him.

'Thanks. Maybe you can deal with these while I sort out the car.' He set the bags on the table.

The bags contained a selection of still-warm Danish pastries, ripe nectarines, a pot of Greek yoghurt and two paper cups of coffee. And a single red rose.

'What's this for?' she asked when he came back in.

He smiled. 'I was going to get you a proper bouquet, but I thought you might refuse it. Whereas a single rose… it's what you'd have on a breakfast tray, and I brought you breakfast. Just without the tray.'

She couldn't help smiling at him. 'Thank you. Though I can't believe you brought take-out coffee. Or, in fact, *any* of this,' she said. She rested her hands on her hips. 'Unlike you, Mr Smith, I happen to keep a properly stocked fridge. I could've provided breakfast.'

He inspected her fridge. 'OK, Ms Bennett. So the food police would give you a gold star and me a compliance notice. But sometimes it's fun to have a takeaway breakfast. And this coffee's excellent.'

He cut one of the nectarines into slices, and juice pooled on the plate. He grinned. 'Good. This is even better than I hoped.'

'How do you mean?'

He fed her a slice, making sure that a tiny rivulet of juice ran down from the corner of her mouth. Then he leaned forward and licked the juice away.

Alexandra was speechless and wide-eyed by the time they'd finished breakfast. And there was no way her legs were going to hold her up.

'Result,' he drawled.

She blew out a breath. 'You don't play fair. This was meant to be just breakfast.'

He shrugged. 'Sometimes you have to push the boundaries.'

And he was definitely pushing hers.

'So what are we going to do today?' he asked.

'I don't know. I...' Her voice faded.

'Can't think straight?' he asked softly.

'No,' she admitted.

'That makes two of us. Remember that day by the river, when you said you hadn't been to the sea for years? We could do that, if you like.'

'What, now? There are all the breakfast things to sort out.'

'They're not going anywhere,' he said. 'They can wait until later. The sunshine can't. Let's go to the sea.'

The Jordan she'd got to know at work was a planner, who'd thought through every possibility before he made a move. This man—spontaneous, playful—was a hell of a lot more dangerous. And he'd thought about what *she* wanted to do. Put her first. Which completely bulldozed her resistance.

'Seriously?' she checked.

He smiled. 'Seriously. What do you need? Flat shoes?'

'And a towel.'

He raised an eyebrow. 'You're planning to *paddle*? In March?'

Yes, and hopefully the coolness of the water at this time of year would help to bring her common sense back. 'How can you resist a paddle at the seaside on a sunny day like this?' she asked. 'The water's going to be gorgeous.'

He smiled, his eyes crinkling at the corners. 'Go and get your stuff, then.'

Alexandra had looked put out at the idea of leaving the breakfast things. Jordan quickly ran some hot water into the bowl, added detergent and dealt with the washing up while he waited for her to get ready. He could hear her humming, 'Oh I Do Like to be Beside the Seaside' as she got her things together, and it made him smile. This was the Alexandra he remembered, sweet and funny and so good to be with.

They'd both been through bad times. Now maybe it was time to have some fun. Although she still wasn't talking to him about her marriage—so he still didn't know what had gone wrong—he'd already worked out that her ex had hurt her badly. Maybe that was why she'd become a workaholic. Pretty much for the same reasons that he had: feeling that he'd failed in his personal life, and work was the only place where he really shone.

The little she had said was that Bennett had swept her off her feet at first. That she'd thought he'd look after her. And then that she'd had to account for every penny she'd spent. Which told Jordan that nobody had really made Alexandra feel special or been the thoughtful, romantic lover she'd dreamed of.

Last time, he'd let her down. Maybe this time he could get it right and be the man she wanted. A man who'd make her feel beautiful and special—not by what he bought her, but by how he treated her.

'Jordan, I didn't expect you to clean my kitchen,' she said when she came back in, carrying a tote bag. 'You didn't have to do that.'

He flapped a dismissive hand at her. 'All I did was wash up a couple of plates and knives. There wasn't that much to do.'

'Thank you, anyway.'

'Let's go.' He waited for her to lock the front door, then ushered her over to his car.

She skated her fingers over the edge of the sleek dark-blue bonnet. 'I still can't get over your flash car.'

'Hey, I'm allowed a vice or two.' And this was his only real indulgence.

'Why don't you drive it to work? No car-park space?'

'I live near enough to walk in. It clears my head in the mornings and puts me in a good mood. Endorphins.'

'We took a taxi back from the store to your place, last night,' she mused.

'Only because I couldn't wait long enough to walk you back.' He smiled wryly. 'And I also couldn't trust myself not to pin you to every wall on the way home and get us both arrested for public indecency.'

She flushed. 'Um.'

He unlocked the car. 'Sorry. I shouldn't have said that. Get in.'

She put her bag on the back seat, then settled herself in the front next to him.

He indicated the sound system. 'Put whatever you want on the radio.'

'Thanks.' She chose a commercial station playing the kind of pop music you could sing along to, then settled back to enjoy the drive.

Once they were round the M25, he headed south.

'So where are we going?' she asked.

'Brighton's the easiest beach to get to from London,' he said. 'Is that OK with you, or would you prefer to go some-where else?' He had the feeling that Bennett had made all the decisions—and she was clearly over-compensating now by being so independent—so he was careful to give her the choice. Especially as Brighton was bound to bring back memories for her, just as it did for him.

'I haven't been to Brighton for years,' she said. 'Not since we…'

He reached over to squeeze her hand briefly. 'Alex, I know it all went wrong, but we had some good times as well.'

Yeah. 'I remember.' The weekend after her eighteenth birthday, they'd spent the Saturday in Brighton. Paddling in the sea, enjoying the rides on the pier, sharing fish and chips on the pebbly beach. And then Jordan had driven her back to London, with his left hand resting on her thigh whenever he didn't need to change gear. The heat and desire had built and built and built, because she'd known exactly what was going to happen.

Thank God her parents had been out.

They'd gone straight up to her room, ripped each other's clothes off—and made love properly for the very first time.

The sound of the sea, the taste of salt in the air, always made her think of that day.

'Alex.' His voice was husky and he let his hand rest on her thigh for just a moment. Telling her without words that he remembered, too.

The nearer they got to the sea, the more she wondered. Was he deliberately trying to recreate that day. Or was this…?

'Stop thinking,' he said softly. 'Today is just you and me and fun, OK?'

'OK.'

* * *

'Shall we start with the pier?' Jordan asked when he'd parked the car.

'Sure.'

He reached for her hand as they walked along the pier; to his relief, she didn't pull away. This was like being a teenager all over again. In some ways, it was unnerving; in others, it was remarkably freeing. Today was all about having fun and forgetting the mess of the past.

'How brave are you feeling?' he asked as they reached the end of the pier.

'How do you mean?'

He indicated the thrill rides. Years ago, she'd always ducked out of them, too scared to go on them. 'Come on, Alex. It'll be fun. Let yourself go.'

She gave him an insolent shrug. 'Lay on, MacDuff,' she quipped.

He bought tokens and they queued up for the roller coaster. When they went through the vertical loop, Alexandra gripped his hand tightly, but she didn't scream the way that some of the other passengers on the cars were screaming. He could see how white her knuckles were, though. And when he glanced at her face he could see that her jaw was clenched. Her entire face was rigid; it was clear that she was absolutely petrified.

He'd hoped that she'd give in to the sheer thrill of the ride, let the adrenalin pump through her and then let herself go with him—but he'd miscalculated badly. 'You hated that, didn't you?' he asked, noting that her legs were slightly wobbly when they got off the ride, and slid his arm round her shoulders to support her.

'I'm OK.'

No, she wasn't. Her voice was shaking, and she was clearly trying to be brave and pretend that she was fine. The roller coaster had obviously terrified her past the ability to scream. He looked regretfully at the ride promising a full-on G-force experience in a matter of seconds. He would have loved to do it, but he knew she wouldn't; and it wouldn't be fair to make her join him on something that extreme. 'Let's do something a bit more traditional. How about an ice cream and that paddle you wanted?' he suggested.

She looked grateful. 'Sounds good to me.'

Alexandra had noticed the speculative look on Jordan's face when he'd seen the newest thrill ride at the end of the pier. No way could she have handled that; and he'd clearly realised it, suggesting that they move off the pier and do something else.

She'd thought that she could handle the roller coaster. But she'd never been on one as terrifying as that one— one where you actually had to go through a loop-the-loop. *Upside down.* She was just glad that Jordan wasn't teasing her about being so feeble; he was being nice, and not making a big issue about it.

She stopped at the beginning of the steeply shelving pebble beach and took off her shoes, then allowed him to hold her hand again as they headed down to the sea. Once at the shoreline, she rolled her jeans up to the knees, put her shoes in her tote bag, and stepped into the water, drawing in a sharp intake of breath as the cool water lapped round her ankles.

'Cold?' he asked.

It was March. What did he expect? 'Actually, it's good. Come on in—the water's lovely,' she said with a grin.

He shook his head. 'You're mad.'

'And you're chicken,' she retorted. 'It's practically summer.'

'What, with spring blossom only just coming out everywhere?' But all the same he took his shoes and socks off, rolled his jeans up and stood at the edge of the sea.

Thought he was going to get out of it, did he? A mischievous impulse made her bend down, scoop up some water in her cupped palms, and fling it at him.

'Oh, my God, that's *cold*!' And then an equally wicked look lit his eyes. 'Right. You asked for it.' He marched straight into the sea, scooped up some water himself, and aimed it straight at her, soaking her T-shirt across her breasts. He tipped his head to one side, surveying his handiwork. 'Mmm.' A grin spread across his face. 'I'd give you first place in a wet T-shirt competition.'

Her face flamed as she realised just what effect the cold water had had on her body. And why he was looking so appreciative: her T-shirt was clinging to her. 'I only splashed you a little bit. *That* was a declaration of war.' She chopped her arm into the water, soaking his jeans up to his thighs.

'War it most definitely is.' He whooped, and a full-scale splashing contest began, ending only when they were both soaked.

'Um, I don't suppose you brought any spare clothes with you?' he asked.

'No.'

'We could go and buy some.'

She shook her head. 'They'll never let us through the door of a shop, looking like this.'

'Guess we'll have to dry out in the sun.' He took her hand and walked up the steep pebbled slope. 'Sorry. I went too far.'

'No, it was fun. I can't remember the last time I had a water fight.'

'I believe we have some new water pistols coming in to the toy department this week. They really need testing by a member of staff,' he mused. 'How about it? You, me, Hampstead Heath and a water fight, next weekend?'

'Regressed to being fourteen, have we?' she teased.

'Yep.' He moved closer so he could whisper in her ear, 'Apart from the fact that I don't have to imagine what you'd look like when I peel that T-shirt off you.'

She went hot all over. 'Behave.'

'Sure.' He spread her towel out on the pebbles, waited for her to settle herself, then stretched out next to her. 'Perfect. You, me, the sun and the sound of the sea.'

'Don't forget the gulls.'

'No.' He propped himself up on one elbow. 'I'm sorry I scared you on the roller coaster.'

She shrugged. 'I'm a wuss.'

'No. I just wanted…I guess, for you to be full of adrenalin and just let go with me today.'

She shifted onto her side so she could face him. 'I don't need a roller coaster for that.'

He looked interested. 'What would make you let go with me, Alex?'

She smiled. 'You were the one pointing out attributes for a wet T-shirt competition.'

His gaze grew hot. 'Were you thinking of getting me naked?'

'No. I was…' She stopped, feeling her face heat. She wasn't sharing *those* thoughts—the picture in her head of Jordan rising from the water, soaking wet and dressed like Mr Darcy in the film that she and Meggie had watched more times than she could remember.

'Penny for them?' he asked.

'Nope.'

He dipped his head so his mouth was close to her ear. 'You'll tell me later.' He nipped her earlobe gently. 'I'll seduce you into it. And that, Alex, is a promise I intend to enjoy keeping.'

'Yeah?' she challenged.

'Yeah.' He stole a kiss. Then he groaned, dipped his head again, and kissed her properly. A kiss that promised as much as it demanded.

She was near to losing it completely. 'Jordan, this is a family beach.'

'And I wish to hell it was private. Because right now I want you naked, with me inside you,' he whispered back.

She could just imagine them on a private beach. Nobody around, just the two of them drying off from the sea. And there would be no reason to stop when he kissed her, touched her...

A moan of need escaped her. 'Are you trying to drive me crazy? Because you're succeeding.'

'You're right. It's a family beach.' He sighed. 'And you look like a really, really sexy mermaid. This is hopeless. You'll have to handcuff me to something so I don't touch you.'

That put even more pictures in her head. She groaned. 'I'm going to be thinking of that all day, now. Sometimes, Jordan Smith...'

'It's an hour and a half back to London.'

'And no way are you going to let us sit in your precious car while we're soaked in sea water.'

'I could get the car valeted.' He stole a kiss. 'But actually, we can lie here and dry off in the sun. Be patient.'

And go quietly insane in the meantime. 'I need distracting. From you,' she clarified.

His eyes lit. 'How about the G-Force thing?'

'Uh—no.'

He smiled. 'I was teasing. I think fish and chips might be a better idea.'

Except it didn't distract them; they ended up feeding chips to each other, tasting each other and stoking their desire to fever point.

Even another paddle—this time without a water fight—didn't manage to cool them down.

'I don't care if we're still wet and I don't care about my car,' Jordan said, pulling her close. 'We're going back to London. Now.'

CHAPTER NINE

How he got them back to London without getting a speeding ticket, she'd never know. But somehow he did, and he parked as close to her door as he could.

He kissed her on the back of her neck as she opened her front door, and desire surged through her. 'Jordan,' she gasped.

They just about made it to her bedroom.

Jordan closed the curtains, then came to stand behind her, wrapping his arms round her waist and hauling her back against him. Even through their clothes, she could feel the warmth of his body against hers. It wasn't enough. She wanted to feel his mouth against her skin, his hands. She wanted everything.

'Jordan. Touch me,' she invited, her voice husky. 'Before I go insane.'

'Touch you.' His hand was splayed across her ribcage; slowly, he moved it upwards until he was cupping one breast. 'Here?'

The breath hissed from her. 'Yes.'

His thumb and forefinger teased her nipple through the fabric of her T-shirt. 'Alex.' His voice sounded husky, lower than usual. He traced a path of kisses along the nape of her neck. 'I want you.'

'Do something about it, then.'

He nibbled the curve between her neck and her shoulder. 'What a good idea.' He slid his fingers underneath the hem of her T-shirt and slowly peeled it off her. Then he reached round to cup her breast properly. 'Oh, yes. The perfect fit,' he whispered huskily, teasing her nipple through the lace of her bra.

Her heartbeat kicked. She wanted him so badly, she was going to implode.

'Turn round,' he said, and dealt with the button and zip of her jeans. He dropped to his haunches as he helped her out of the denims, then nuzzled her abdomen while he undid the clip of her bra and let the lace fall to the floor. 'Mmm. I like having you like this.'

'Practically naked, while you're fully dressed?' she asked.

He laughed and threw her earlier words back at him. 'Do something about it, then.'

'Me?' She smiled. 'No. I have a much better idea.' She went and sat cross-legged on the bed. 'Why don't you undress for me?'

'Strip for you?' His eyes lit with amusement. 'If that's what you want.'

'It is.'

He undressed so slowly that Alexandra was close to climbing off the bed and ripping the rest of his clothes off—but patience was a virtue, she reminded herself, and she was most definitely going to get her reward.

At last, he was completely naked. And utterly beautiful.

He joined her on the bed. 'Alex. I'm not sure whether I want to start by touching you, tasting you, or just looking at you.' He reached out to touch her shoulder, smoothed the flat of his palm down over her upper arms. 'Your skin's so soft, so smooth—so perfect. And you're all curves. Gorgeous, feminine curves.'

He shifted so that he was kneeling before her, and cupped her breasts. 'Perfect,' he whispered huskily. 'The perfect size, the perfect shape...You feel wonderful.' He rubbed the pad of his thumb across her nipples, making them peak and harden under his touch. 'And I need to taste you, Alex.' He took one nipple into his mouth, teasing it with his tongue.

His mouth was hot against her skin, and Alexandra could feel her temperature rising. 'Jordan.' She slid her hands into his hair, urging him on, and closed her eyes so she could concentrate on the sensations washing through her.

In one fluid movement, he moved them both so that she was lying back against the pillows. He kissed his way down over her belly, then gently parted her legs and kissed her inner thigh. He pulled the lace of her knickers to one side, and she felt his tongue glide along the folds of her sex.

She gasped as he found her clitoris and teased it with the tip of his tongue; her arousal deepened, spiralling within her and spreading need through every nerve end. 'Oh, God, yes, Jordan—yes. Please.' She didn't care that she was begging, now. She needed the release so badly. He'd teased her all day, and she was so hot for him.

After the last awful year of her marriage, when Nathan had insisted on scheduling sex purely during the most fertile phase of her cycle, with the sole aim of making babies, it felt amazing to be making love with a man purely because he wanted to make love with her. Because he wanted to give her pleasure, and take pleasure in return.

And it was as if Jordan could read her mind; he continued to pleasure her, sliding one finger inside her to ease the ache and flicking the tip of his tongue rapidly across her clitoris, varying the speed and pressure until she couldn't even remember where she was any more.

Her climax hit unexpectedly, intense and sharp, and she gasped his name and went still. He held her while the aftershocks bubbled through her, then shifted to lie beside her.

'Right now,' he said, 'I really want to be inside you.' He kissed her lightly, retrieved his wallet and removed a condom.

He was kneeling between her thighs again; he still hadn't bothered removing her knickers, and simply pushed the material to one side. She felt the tip of his penis nudge against her entrance—and then he was inside her with one long, slow, deep thrust.

The perfect fit.

He rolled onto his back, taking her with him. 'You're in charge,' he said softly.

So different from the way it had been in her marriage, when Nathan was always in charge. When he'd always insisted on the same position: the one that, according to him, was the best one for conception.

And she found she loved being in charge, setting the pace. His hands were gripping the pillow tightly as she raised and lowered herself over him, taking it so slowly that he was almost whimpering, then speeding up until he was gasping her name.

In his eyes, she could see the exact moment that his climax hit—the moment when her body started to tighten round him, pleasure rippling through her over and over, tipping him into his own release. He moved to a sitting position, wrapping his arms round her and holding her close; she could feel his heart thudding hard and fast, slowly settling down as his climax ebbed away.

He went to the bathroom, then came back to bed, drawing her back into his arms so her head was pillowed on his shoulder and her fingers were linked with his, resting across his heart.

'So are you going to tell me what you were thinking about? When you went all dreamy?'

'You as Mr Darcy. Wet. Emerging from the pool.' The words slipped out before she could stop them.

'That can be arranged,' he said. His eyes glittered with amusement. 'And I guess that would be fitting, Ms Bennet.'

'With two Ts, in my case. And it's Alexandra, not Elizabeth.'

'Alexandra's a prettier name.' He kissed her lightly. 'Why did you keep his name?'

The question was straight out of left field—and so unexpected that she blurted out the truth. 'I'm not Alex Porter any more. I'm not that naïve, innocent teenager.'

'He hurt you, Alex,' Jordan said softly. 'Did he hit you?'

'No.' It had been much more subtle than that. All smiles when she did what he wanted, and cold criticism when she didn't. 'I guess,' she said, 'it's to remind myself.'

He said nothing, simply held her. And that gave her the courage to finish the sentence. 'To remind myself never to let anyone control me again.'

Jordan hated seeing the pain in her eyes. 'That sounds like a very hard lesson.'

She nodded. 'It was.'

'I'm sorry you had to go through that. How did you meet him?'

'At the bus stop. It was raining, my umbrella broke, and he offered to share his.'

Looking after her, Jordan thought. He would've made

the same offer if someone in the queue next to him had had the same problem.

'He asked me out to dinner that night.'

Jordan felt a flicker of jealousy, but tried hard not to show it. Now she'd started opening up to him, he didn't want to make her clam up again. Especially as he had a feeling that this was something she almost never talked about. Maybe not even to her best friend, Meggie.

Clearly Nathan Bennett had been a charmer, because back then Meggie had been one of the most spiky and sus- picious people Jordan had ever met—and she'd seemed to approve of Bennett. He could still remember the words she'd flung at him when he asked her where Alex was. *She's married to someone who'll treat her properly.*

How wrong they'd all been.

'I turned him down.' Alexandra's brown eyes were huge. 'I didn't think I could ever face getting involved with anyone again, after you. But he asked me the next day, too. And then I started thinking, why shouldn't I? And he was *nice*, Jordan. He made me feel special, swept me off my feet. He did all the little chivalrous things like holding doors open for me, holding my chair out, bring- ing me flowers.'

All the things *he* should've been doing for her.

'He was eighteen years older than me, but the age dif- ference didn't matter.'

Twice her age, Jordan thought. And that kind of age difference mattered when you hadn't quite finished grow- ing up. Alexandra had still had years of change ahead of her—which didn't bode well for her marriage.

'I guess I thought he'd look after me,' she said softly. 'That he'd support me, the way you and my parents didn't.'

Jordan flinched inwardly, but he knew he deserved that. From her point of view, he hadn't been there. He hadn't supported her—though only because he hadn't known the truth.

'But he didn't.'

'No. And…' She blew out a breath. 'I don't want to talk about him, right now.'

She'd already told him much more than she'd told him before. She'd let him closer to her. And although he really wanted to know the rest, so he could wipe the shadows out of her life, he knew that now wasn't the time to ask. He didn't want to risk making her back away again. 'OK. Let's change the subject.' He paused. 'Are you going to ask me to stay the night?'

'I don't think that's a good idea,' she said carefully.

The last time she'd said something was a bad idea, she'd let him persuade her into it. Though this needed to be her choice, not pressure from him. He needed to show her that he wasn't like Bennett. He wasn't going to try to control her. He stole a kiss. 'Would that be in the slightest bit negotiable?'

'No.'

And it sounded as if she was already backing away. Although it was a bitter disappointment—he wanted the teasing, playful Alex who'd started a water fight in the sea—he knew that this wasn't the time to push her too hard. 'OK. I'll take your lead on that. But will you at least have breakfast with me tomorrow?'

She frowned. 'But you had today off. Aren't you going to be catching up in the office tomorrow?'

'Not first thing. Though I am supposed to be going to my parents' for lunch.' He stroked her face. 'Maybe you could come with me—if you'd like to, that is.'

'I don't think your mother would be too pleased at that idea.'

'Actually, I think she would.'

Alexandra scoffed. 'Considering what she said to me the last time we met, I'm not buying that.'

'She was horrified when I told her what really happened back then. Really upset. And she's been trying to work out how she can get to see you and apologise properly. Lunch would be a start.'

Alexandra sat bolt upright as his words sank in. 'You *told* her?'

'She was wrong about you, and I needed to put her straight.'

Some of her fears must've shown on her face, because he added, 'Don't worry, she's not going to be broadcasting your private business to everyone she knows.' He held her close. 'She jumped to conclusions and thought the worst.'

'You're telling me.' Alexandra couldn't quite keep the bitterness from her voice.

'You and I did that too—so, although she was completely in the wrong, you and I don't exactly have any high moral ground to stand on between us.'

She felt her eyes narrow. 'I'm not a gold-digger, Jordan. I never was.'

'I know that. She knows that, too.' He stroked her face. 'I learned something else I'd never known before—something that she gave me permission to share with you. The reason I'm an only child isn't because my parents were workaholics. My mother had four miscarriages after me, and after that work was the only thing that kept her sane.'

Alexandra froze. Jordan's mother hadn't been able to have more children.

She knew how that felt. She couldn't even have *one*.

Did it mean that Vanessa was putting pressure on Jordan to give her grandchildren? Did Jordan want children? It was something she was going to have to face; and it would be easier on both of them if she found out now. So she could back away before they got in too deep. 'You said about getting married and settling down when your father was ill. Did that include having children?' she asked carefully.

'Lindsey and I didn't get to that stage.'

'But you want children?'

'It's not something I've thought about very much,' he said. 'When my marriage went wrong, I concentrated on work. Though I admit, since you've been back in my life, I've thought about it. Especially at that first story-time session, seeing you with the children. Our baby would've been ten years old, now. And it made me think maybe there would've been a brother or sister in Meggie's class, someone who took part in making that banner.'

She swallowed hard, willing the tears to stay back. If things had been different, if she hadn't lost the baby... She wouldn't have failed her exams or left home, Jordan would've come to find her and discovered the truth, and together they could've worked something out. She would never have met Nathan. Never have had that second ectopic pregnancy. Never have...

'Alex?' He brushed a gentle kiss against her mouth.

'I need some time.' Time to absorb what he'd told her. Time to think about where this was going, what she wanted—what *he* wanted.

'OK. I'll take the hint and go home.' He held her gaze. 'But one thing I want you to be sure about. I'm not Bennett and I never will be. This thing between us—wherever it goes, whatever happens, I want it to be on equal terms.'

She managed a shaky smile. 'So tomorrow it's my turn to bring breakfast to you?'

'If that's what you'd like to do. It doesn't mean you have

to. I can go to the supermarket on my way home tonight and stock my fridge properly.'

This time, her laugh was genuine. 'When do you ever go to the supermarket? Your kitchen's full of takeaway menus, with a few bits of fruit stuck in a bowl on the worktop to make it look as if you eat healthily.'

'I do eat healthily. I just don't happen to cook what I eat, that's all.' He climbed out of bed and dressed swiftly. 'You don't have to get up to see me out. Stay there. You look cute. And comfortable.' He stole a last kiss. 'See you tomorrow. And remember, we're just doing the simple stuff right now.'

The simple stuff, Alexandra thought as she heard the door close behind him. Why did she have the nasty feeling that it was just going to start getting complicated?

When Jordan opened his front door to Alexandra the next morning, he was wearing a pair of faded, close-fitting denims. And nothing else.

It made her mouth water and her pulse race. She couldn't help looking him up and down. God, the man even had sexy *feet*. Everything about him made her want to rip off the few clothes he was wearing and drag him off to bed.

'Do you always answer your door looking like that?' she asked.

'If I happen to know it's you…maybe.' He kissed her lingeringly. 'Good morning. And it's a much better morning now that you're here. You brought the sunshine with you.'

She laughed. 'Jordan, it's raining on and off.' She'd got caught in a shower, walking here from the Tube station. Just to prove it, she shook her wet hair, so droplets of rain splashed over his bare chest.

He laughed back. 'It *feels* sunny. Even if it is wet outside.' His eyes lit up. 'Are you suggesting another water fight?'

'No.' She handed him the paper bags. 'Breakfast, as promised.'

He peeked inside the first one. 'What do we have here? Oh, nice. Proper butter, posh jam, warm croissants...' He raised an eyebrow. 'But I smell no coffee.'

'Other bag,' she said.

He looked inside and frowned. 'What's this?'

'A pack of proper coffee.' She paused. 'I assume you *do* possess a cafetière? And milk?'

'Yes to the milk, no to the cafetière,' he said cheerfully. 'I usually drink decaf instant at home. It's quicker.'

'OK, we'll improvise.' She was good at thinking on her feet. 'Do you have a tea strainer?'

'Nope.'

She shook her head. 'How can you get to thirty years old and not even have the basics in your kitchen, Jordan?'

He shrugged. 'Because I don't cook. If I hold a dinner party, it's at a restaurant.'

Maybe, Alexandra thought, Lindsey had taken most of the kitchenware when she'd left. Jordan's flat definitely felt more like a bachelor pad than the family home pared down. 'OK. Decaf instant it is.' And she was *so* buying him a cafetière. The deli at Field's sold thirty different types of coffee, and she intended to try every single one. Preferably with him. And not as a marketing exercise: just for fun.

She busied herself setting things out on the table. He came to stand behind her, slid his arms round her waist and drew her back against him. He nuzzled the neck of her long-sleeved T-shirt out of the way and kissed her bare skin. 'Now you know the real reason why I buy take-out coffee in the mornings.'

'Uh-huh.'

'*And* you brought the Sunday papers with you, you wonderful woman.' He nibbled her earlobe. 'How do you fancy breakfast in bed?'

She turned round to face him. 'That depends on how persuasive you are.'

He laughed. 'Now that's a challenge I'm going to enjoy.'

Ten minutes later, she was naked and in his bed.

Half an hour after that, he reheated the croissants in the microwave, made them both a mug of coffee, and brought a tray in, with the newspapers tucked under his arm.

They fed each other croissants, except butter kept dripping onto their skin and needing to be licked off. Licking led to kissing, kissing led to touching, and the coffee was cold before they got round to drinking it.

'I'll make some more,' he said.

'No, it's fine—if I'm busy I sometimes forget to drink my coffee until it's cold,' she said.

'That's so uncivilised, Alex.'

She kissed him lingeringly. 'Maybe I just don't want you to get out of bed. I'm warm and I'm comfortable. Stay put,' she invited softly. 'Please?'

'Since you asked so nicely, sure.' His eyes crinkled at the corners, and he settled back against the pillows.

Alexandra thoroughly enjoyed lazing the morning away in bed with Jordan and the newspaper. Tackling the cryptic crossword with him, laughing over the answers, and feeling slightly smug when she solved an anagram before he did.

Eventually, he sighed. 'I have to go. Have you thought any more about coming with me?'

'I'm not ready, Jordan.' She took a deep breath. 'But I appreciate the olive branch. Can you apologise for me?'

'Sure.'

'Thank you. Give me three minutes to get dressed, and I'll be out of your hair,' she said.

'Did you drive over?' He looked horrified. 'I forgot to ask—you might have a parking ticket by now. If you do, I'll pay the fine.'

'Don't worry.' She smiled at him. 'I don't have a car. I took the Tube.'

'Then I'll give you a lift back.'

'No, you're late already. I'll be fine.'

'So what are you going to do for the rest of the day? Go and see your parents?'

Hardly. She couldn't even remember the last time she'd spoken to them on the phone, let alone seen them. Probably her father's birthday. The rift between them had grown wider and wider over the years—firstly with her leaving home, hurt by their lack of support, and Nathan hadn't encouraged her to mend the rift. It had suited his purposes for her to be more reliant on him. *You don't need anyone else. Only me.* And as her confidence had eroded she'd come to believe him.

Until one of her clients had made her take a long, hard look at her life.

But her parents hadn't tried to get closer to her after the divorce. And she'd learned that she was better off just relying on herself and a couple of close friends. Friends who would no doubt think she needed her head examining for getting involved with Jordan Smith again.

'No,' she said. 'I think I'm going to wander round the V&A for a couple of hours. And then I'm going home to watch a really girly film. And then I'm going to cook myself a risotto.'

'Would there be enough for two?' he asked, looking hopeful.

It was tempting, but she'd already spent too much time

with him this weekend for her own peace of mind. 'No. Go and see your parents,' she said. She softened her words with a kiss. 'I'll do the washing up before I go.'

'Leave it. I'll do it later.' He kissed her back. 'Enjoy your museum.'

Rather than going back to her flat, she went straight to the Victoria & Albert Museum in Kensington. Though as she wandered round her attention was snagged away from the exhibits; she was acutely aware of the other visitors to the museum. Nobody seemed to be on their own. They were either in couples, in family groups, or in a group of friends.

Right at that moment, she really missed Jordan and she was cross with herself for feeling that way. She absolutely couldn't allow herself to fall for him. Hadn't he broken her heart badly enough last time? And she'd promised herself after the misery of her marriage that she'd never let her heart get involved again. That she'd protect herself from all the pain of a broken relationship. Ever since then, she'd kept everyone at a slight distance, even friends. So why was she being so reckless now?

Alexandra wasn't in the best of moods when she got back to her flat, and although the film was one of her favourites she found herself drifting off into her thoughts partway through. Even the risotto seemed tasteless, and she ended up putting most of it in the bin.

Funny how the world seemed smaller and two-dimensional without Jordan around.

And she was the biggest fool in the world for letting herself think like this. She'd just spent a perfectly nice afternoon doing something she enjoyed. So what if it was on her own? She didn't need a man to make her life complete. And she most definitely didn't need Jordan Smith.

* * *

Later that evening, Jordan called. 'Hi. Just checking to see if there was any leftover risotto?'

'No. And don't try to con me that your mother didn't feed you.'

'She fed me.' He sighed. 'Though I would much rather have gone to the museum with you.'

'Maybe, but you would've hated the film.'

'How do you know? Maybe I like girly films.'

She laughed. 'Now you're *really* trying to con me.'

'I probably wouldn't have been paying enough attention for you to grill me on the plot or what have you afterwards,' he admitted. 'But I would've been quite happy to keep you company. You, me, your sofa…Now that sounds good.'

'Maybe next weekend.'

'I can work with maybe. See you tomorrow,' he said softly. 'Sleep well.'

Over the next three weeks, Jordan found himself getting much closer to Alexandra. He was careful to be completely professional with her at work, when anyone else was around, though he sent her the occasional text to make her blush and laugh. And when she realised that he meant it about giving her a choice and not insisting on choosing every film they saw and every place they went, she seemed to relax with him more.

She'd even bought him a cafetière, wrapping it up in white tissue paper and tying a deep red ribbon round it, then teasing him about his lack of domestication when he unwrapped it. They had breakfast together at the weekends, and they'd fallen into the habit of alternating an evening meal at the trattoria with a meal at her place. He enjoyed pottering round in her kitchen, just watching her cook.

But the one thing she consistently refused to do was to

spend the night with him. No matter how late it was, she insisted either on going home or sending him home. And he really wanted to break that last barrier between them, to wake up in the morning with her in his arms. For her to be the first thing he saw when he woke.

Maybe, Jordan thought, he needed to take her somewhere that had no memories for them. Somewhere he knew she really wanted to go—and then when they got back really, really late she might decide to stay over for once.

The following Friday night, he told her, 'I'm going to take you on a mystery tour tomorrow.'

'Mystery?' She smiled at him. 'Sounds fun. What's the dress code?'

'Smart-casual. Oh, and shoes you can walk in.'

'Flat shoes.' Her eyes gleamed. 'Is there any chance this might be the seaside?'

'You'll definitely see the sea,' he promised. He just wasn't telling her *which* sea. She didn't need to know that he was thinking of the Adriatic rather than the English Channel. 'I'll pick you up at six tomorrow morning.'

She blinked. 'The crack of dawn?'

'Yes. Oh, and you need your passport.'

'My passport? Why? Have you booked us tickets to Paris, or something?'

He grinned. 'Tut. Someone needs to brush up her geography. Since when has Paris been on the coast?'

'Well, you might be able to see the sea from the train on the way there,' she pointed out.

'We're not going to Paris.'

She frowned. 'So where are we going?'

'I told you—it's a mystery tour.' He stole a kiss. 'You'll find out, tomorrow.'

She kissed him back. 'Tell me now?'

'No.' He waltzed her to her front door and kissed her

again. 'Sleep well.' He knew he wouldn't; he'd be restless and fidgety. But maybe tomorrow night, he would. With Alexandra in his arms.

CHAPTER TEN

JORDAN arrived with a taxi at precisely six o'clock. Despite what he'd said the previous night, Alexandra was still half expecting the taxi to take them to St Pancras to catch the train to Paris; but when they ended up at the airport instead, she was completely thrown. 'Jordan, where are we going?'

He simply smiled. 'All in good time.'

She didn't have a clue until Jordan took her to the check-in desk.

'We're going to Venice, just for the *day*?' she asked in disbelief.

He spread his hands. 'OK, so it's a bit decadent—but if I remember rightly it was top of your wish list after Rome, wasn't it?'

He remembered that? 'Jordan, this is the best surprise ever. I really don't know what to say.'

'My marketing manager, lost for words? That's a first,' he teased. Then his face softened. 'You don't need to say anything, Alex. I wanted to do something nice for you. And I've been panicking all week in case I got this wrong.'

'How can you get Venice wrong? Jordan, it's…' She could feel her eyes filling with tears, but they were happy tears. It was the nicest thing anyone had ever done for her.

Though part of her was panicking. Whenever Nathan

had done something for her, she'd paid for it with a little bit more of her independence.

As if he guessed her thoughts, he said softly, 'Shall I tell you what I'm expecting from today? You, me, and a whole lot of fun. And that's it. No strings attached, no conditions. Just you and me.'

'Thank you.' The words sounded cracked, but she meant them.

He held her hand all the way on the plane.

'So we're going on the *vaporetto* now?' she asked when they'd gone through Customs at the airport.

'Better than that. I booked us a *motoscafo*.'

'Which is, in English?' she prompted.

'A water taxi. Apparently this means we get a fabulous first view of the city—and it's just you and me.' He took her down to the jetty and handed in a docket for the water taxi.

'Wow. The water really *is* turquoise. Just like in all the photos I've seen,' she said as the *motoscafo* brought them into the city. And he'd been right about the *motoscafo*. The views of Venice were amazing. The sunlight glittering brilliant white on the water. The sprawl of houses and bridges and domes and towers, all covered in stucco the colour of ice cream. Ancient buildings with their stucco peeling off and worn exposed brickwork rubbed shoulders with smart, renovated buildings whose windows were protected by ornate ironwork grilles and whose windowboxes were filled with flowers. And, above all of it, there was the bluest sky she'd ever seen.

'*La Serenissima*. Venice, the most serene city,' he said softly.

She sucked in a breath. 'Jordan, this is really special.'

He smiled. 'Isn't it just? And I really wanted to share this with you.' His fingers tightened round hers.

The *motoscafo* took them right down the Grand Canal; gondolas and motor boats were tied up at jetties, and buildings jostled next to each other, five storeys high, with narrow arched windows and stone balustrades picked out in white against deep reds, ochres and golds. Some of the buildings were familiar to her from TV programmes, films and photographs; but, in the flesh, they were even more lovely. She was utterly entranced.

'Oh, wow, and that's the bridge. "What news on the Rialto?"' she quoted.

'Such a romantic setting for the most *un*romantic play Shakespeare ever wrote.'

She laughed. 'Absolutely—oh, Jordan, this is just how I imagined it. No, actually, it's better. I… Thank you so much.' She flung her arms round him and kissed him.

He'd chosen the right place, then. Even behind those sunglasses, he knew her eyes were sparkling. Her face was lit up, and she looked completely thrilled to be here. Just as he'd hoped.

The water-taxi driver moored at the jetty by the Rialto Bridge and helped them both out.

'*Mille grazie,*' Jordan said, leaving him a tip. Then he turned to Alexandra. 'Do you want to go exploring?'

'You bet.'

He took his mobile phone from his pocket and flicked into the book he'd bought the previous evening. 'I thought we could do with a map and a tour guide so we know what we're looking at.'

She looked surprised. 'So you haven't been to Venice before?'

'No.'

'How come?'

Because your ghost would've followed me here. Not that he was going to tell her that.

He shrugged. 'I guess it's one of those things. There are so many places in the world you want to see, you can't do them all at once.'

'I guess not.'

She followed him up the steps of the bridge. The marble nearest to the inside of the bridge was smooth and shiny from years of tourists leaning across it while they admired the view; Alexandra skimmed her fingers across it. 'I wonder how many thousands of people have done this before me?'

'More than either of us could guess. It's a beautiful view,' Jordan said. 'Hey. Indulge me. Lean into the bridge and smile.' He took a photograph of her on his camera. The same photograph that most of the other tourists on the bridge were taking, though it felt as if it were just the two of them there. And she looked so beautiful, with the sunlight glinting on her hair and that wide, wide smile— a smile just for him.

'Do you want me to take one of you?' she asked.

'No, you're fine. Let's go and see the market.'

He took her hand and they wandered over to the other end of the bridge and through narrow side streets. The area opened up unexpectedly to the market place, where stalls were heaped high with produce and shoppers were haggling with the stallholders.

'This is amazing, Jordan.' She stared at the stalls in delight. 'Every fruit and vegetable you can think of, fresh herbs sold by the handful…'

'And these. Wow, just look at these.' He took her over to a stall that sold tiny wild strawberries no bigger than the nail on her little finger, and bought a punnet. 'Alex, close your eyes and open your mouth.'

Despite the fact they were in the middle of a crowded market place, it felt oddly intimate; it sent a kick of desire through him, seeing her eyes closed and her face lifted to his and her lips parted like that. He didn't know whether he wanted to kiss her, first, or feed her the strawberry; she made his head swim.

Be sensible, he told himself. His fingers brushed against her lips as he slid one of the tiny strawberries into her mouth, and every nerve end in his skin tingled at the contact.

'The sweetest thing I've ever tasted,' she said, and then laid her palm against his cheek. 'Except maybe you.'

'Is that a fact?' he drawled.

In response, she grinned. 'Close your eyes.' She teased him by brushing the fruit against his lips and then pulling it away as he reached for it.

He opened his eyes and grabbed her hand. 'You, madam, are not playing fair.'

'I know.' She fed him the strawberry, not looking the slightest bit abashed.

He smiled, loving this teasing, relaxed side of her. 'You're right. The sweetest thing except you.'

She reached up on tiptoe and brushed her mouth against his. 'That's on account.'

'I'll hold you to that.'

'I can't believe we're actually here, in Venice.' She gazed around in wonder. 'Jordan, it's incredible.'

He agreed. Completely. And how glad he was that he'd waited to share this with her. 'Let's go to the fish market,' he said when they'd finished the strawberries.

They followed their noses. 'Wow. I don't think I've ever seen so many kinds of fish in one place before.' Tiny octopuses and spider crabs and grey shrimps, alongside other kinds of fish they couldn't even name. One of the fishmongers tipped a stream of chilled water from a red watering-can onto the display, cooling the fish down and making it glisten invitingly to the shoppers. 'Hey, we could do that at Field's,' she said.

'And you'd get a health order slapped on me straight away. You're not getting that one past me, let alone the Board,' he said.

'Spoilsport,' she teased.

Once they'd had their fill of the market, they bought *gelati* from one of the little kiosks and crossed back over the Rialto Bridge, following the signs for San Marco through the network of paths and narrow stone and wrought iron bridges. They window-shopped along the way; Alexandra exclaimed over the filigree masks, then stopped him by a glass shop.

'Look at this bowl—it's gorgeous. That deep, intense blue shading to the same turquoise as the Venetian lagoon.' She sighed as she looked at the price tag. 'Unfortunately, that's way out of my price range, but our customers might like it.'

'Maybe, but we're not here for work,' he said, surprising himself; he didn't usually think twice about bringing business into his time off. But today was different. Today was just for them, and he resented the idea of anything else intruding. 'We're playing hooky. This is just for you and me. Right now, work doesn't matter.'

She nodded. 'Got it.'

As they walked under the clock tower into St Mark's Square, the onion-shaped domes of the Basilica glittered white against the bluest sky he'd ever seen, and the Doge's Palace was like a beautiful layered pink-and-white wedding cake.

'Just…wow. There really are no words to do this place justice. It's like no other city I've been to,' she said softly.

'And are those the famous bronze horses up there on the balcony of the basilica?'

He consulted the guidebook on his mobile phone. 'Apparently they're reproductions—the original ones are inside.'

'Can we go and see them?'

He smiled at her. 'Sure. That's what today's all about: doing whatever you—*we*,' he corrected himself, 'want and enjoying every second.'

The inside of the basilica took Alexandra's breath away; there were literally thousands of glass tesserae shaped into mosaics, their colours still as bright as the day they were made. She could quite understand why the tourists obeyed the notices asking them not to talk, because they simply wouldn't have words when they saw all this for the first time. She certainly didn't—and neither, it seemed, did Jordan. He just held her hand, his fingers twined through hers.

She paid for their tickets to go up to see the original bronze horses; after sighing over their beauty, they headed out to the loggia to see the reproductions and stood outside in the sunshine, looking over the square and the lagoon.

'I can see why they keep the original inside, to preserve them. But these are perfect reproductions. Utterly beautiful,' she said.

'So are you.' He stole a kiss. 'Stand there. I'll take your picture.'

'Excuse me,' an elderly woman asked. 'Would you like me to take a picture of you together?'

'Yes, please.' She took her mobile phone from her handbag and showed the older woman how the camera worked, then posed with Jordan next to the horses.

'Are you on your honeymoon?' the woman asked.

Alexandra went very still. No, they weren't, and she still wasn't sure where this was going. She was starting to think that she knew where she wanted it to go, but she hadn't told Jordan everything yet. And it scared her that things would change when he knew the truth about her; even though she knew he wasn't like Nathan, things had gone really badly wrong once Nathan realised that she couldn't give him the children he wanted. Would it be the same with Jordan?

Jordan wrapped his arms round her waist and drew her back against his body. 'Sort of,' he said. 'We're not married, but this is a special time for us.'

That much was true; it was a day just for them. For doing what they wanted. No strings and no conditions. The tension seeping out of her, she looked up at him and smiled.

'Venice is the most romantic city in the world,' the older woman said. 'We came here on our honeymoon. My husband can't manage the steps up here now, but we always come back to Venice for our anniversary. And I always look out from here, just as we did on our very first visit.'

'Happy anniversary,' Alexandra said.

'Thank you, my dear. And I hope you both find the same magic we have in Venice.'

Alexandra had a feeling that they might just have done that.

When they'd finished looking round the basilica, they found a little kiosk selling *piadina*, toasted flatbread stuffed with prosciutto and pecorino cheese. A short wander brought them to a bench in a quiet little square overlooking the canal.

'Thank you,' Alexandra said. 'This is really special. I

mean, I loved going to the seaside with you at home, but here...'

'There's nowhere in the world like Venice.' Jordan laced his fingers through hers. 'How about *really* playing hooky?'

'How do you mean?'

'Let's not go back until tomorrow. Let's stay the night.'

'But—Jordan, we don't have anywhere booked. Or anything with us. Or—'

He cut her words off by the simple expedient of kissing her. '"Peace, I will stop your mouth,"' he quoted softly when he broke the kiss.

'Indeed, Signor Benedick,' she responded dryly.

'It's all doable, Alex. I can change our flights to tomorrow afternoon and we can find a hotel. We can buy a change of clothes, and the hotel will have all the toiletries we need.' He drew her hand up to his mouth and kissed it. 'So we get to spend the night in Venice, maybe take a ride on a gondola, have dinner, dance through St Mark's Square when it's all lit up...whatever you fancy doing. How about it?'

'As long as I get to pay my half.'

'You're so stubborn.' He sighed. 'Look, I've got a pretty good idea why you feel that way, but there really aren't any strings attached. I earn more than you do, and it's not fair for you to pay half—that wouldn't be equal. I can afford a hotel room, and I just want to do something nice for you, Alex. Give you some good memories.'

To help wipe out some of the bad ones. And she knew he wasn't like Nathan and wouldn't expect anything from her in return—but she still needed to feel that she'd given him something back. 'How about a compromise?' she suggested. 'We stay in Venice tonight, but you let me take you out to dinner.'

'OK. It's a deal.' He paused. 'So do I book one room or two?'

Since the beginning of their affair, she hadn't let herself spend the night with Jordan, knowing how easy it would be to fall in love with him all over again. Not actually sleeping with him was the only way she could think of to retain some kind of distance between them.

But this was Venice. And, as he'd said to the woman who'd taken their photograph by the bronze horses, this was a special time for them. Time to be together without any pressures. No past, no future: just the present. She could allow herself tonight. Just tonight, to fall asleep in his arms and wake up next to him in the morning.

'One.'

'Are you sure about that?'

She swallowed hard. 'I'm sure.'

He brushed his mouth lightly against hers. 'I promise you won't regret that. Give me a moment.' He grabbed his phone from his pocket and looked something up on the Internet, then made two calls—one of which was in rapid Italian and she couldn't follow it.

'OK,' he said when he cut the connection. 'We have a room, and our flights have been changed to tomorrow afternoon. And I think we need to go shopping.'

While Alexandra was trying on a little black dress and high-heeled shoes, Jordan spotted a pendant shaped like a starfish in turquoise glass, shading to intense blue and laced with silver. He knew she'd love it—both the colours and the style—so he bought it and slipped it in his pocket.

Then he went over to her cubicle. 'Alex?'

'Yes?' Her voice was faintly muffled.

'Do I get to see what you look like?'

Her face appeared round the curtain. 'Are you saying you want to choose my dress?'

'No.' He bent closer. 'I'm saying I'd like to see you try the clothes on.'

'A private show?' She blushed. 'Not here.'

She wasn't saying no. Just not here. 'Where, then?'

'The hotel.'

He stole a kiss. 'I'm so going to hold you to that.'

Her blush deepened. 'Jordan. I hope the assistants don't speak good enough English to know what you just said.'

He had a feeling that they wouldn't need a translation. The way he felt about Alexandra was written all over his face, in letters a mile high. He brushed another kiss against her mouth. 'OK, I'll behave and wait outside. Take your time. No rush.'

Eventually she emerged with an expensive-looking carrier bag. 'So that's something for tonight, something clean for tomorrow, clean underwear…and I think we're going to need a small suitcase to get this stuff back to England.'

'Something small enough for hand luggage. It'll save hanging around by the carousel when we're back in England,' he said.

It didn't take long to find a suitable case.

Then he handed her the box. 'For you.'

She looked taken aback. 'For me?'

'I thought it might go with your dress.'

She opened the box and her eyes widened. 'Jordan, it's beautiful, but you didn't have to buy me anything.'

He sighed. Her independence drove him crazy; since she'd opened up to him about Nathan, he could understand why, but she knew he wasn't like her ex. And she was taking the independence thing way too far. 'Alex, it wasn't that expensive. Besides, you're my girlfriend. Which means I'm allowed to buy you jewellery.'

She actually flinched.

'Alex?'

'No. Ignore me.' She shook her head. 'I'll shut up. Thank you, Jordan. It's gorgeous.'

What had made her flinch like that? She'd said before that she'd had to account for every penny. Had she bought herself some jewellery and her husband had been furious about it?

Part of him didn't want to push her, in case she put up the barriers again. But part of him knew that this was a wound that needed lancing. Giving her time to brood would put a shadow over a day he wanted to be filled with sunshine.

'Come on. We've been walking for ages. We need a sit-down and a coffee,' he said. He found a *caffè*, ordered them both a cappuccino, and then found them a quiet corner where they could sit down and talk without being overheard.

'You're going to ask, aren't you?' she said, looking miserable.

'Yup.'

She sighed. 'I guess I owe you the truth.'

'You don't owe me anything,' he said softly. 'And I can assure you now that whatever you say isn't going any further than me. But maybe telling me might help you—because I get the impression you've bottled an awful lot of things up. And eventually they're going to have to come out before they hurt you any more.' He reached over and took her hand. 'Was he angry with you for buying yourself something?'

She gave a weary nod. 'We always had to do things his way. I went along with it for a while, because it was nice not to have to be the one making all the decisions, but gradually I started to feel I was losing myself. I couldn't make a decision without wondering what he would think, first. And it made me feel more and more of a failure.' She bit her lip. 'I wanted to retake my A levels. He kept talking me out of it, saying that I didn't need them because I had him and he'd always look after me. But looking after turned into—well, smothering me.'

'Retaking your A levels was something you wanted to do. Something for *you*. Why didn't he support you?'

'I guess he was worried that it was the thin end of the wedge. That I'd start to better myself, so I wouldn't need him any more and I'd leave him.'

He frowned. 'But that's crazy. That's not who you are.'

She gave him a wan smile. 'Thank you. But he couldn't see that. Looking back, I think he was as needy and insecure as I was. And I could've handled it better.'

'You were eighteen, Alex. He had a lot more life experience than you did.'

'Maybe. But I started lying to him, just to give myself some space. I told him I was going out with the girls once a week, and I went to an evening class instead. I guess it wasn't a total lie—one of my friends was taking the same class, so I was sort of going out with one of the girls. But he assumed I was out with a different group of friends, and he assumed I was doing girly stuff instead of studying.'

How desperately sad that she'd been forced into lying, Jordan thought.

'But then one of my friends rang me when I was out at class—and Nathan had thought I was out with her. When I got home, he accused me of having an affair. And when I told him what I'd really been doing...' She shook her head. 'He wasn't any happier about it. That's when he started making me account for every penny I spent. We had a joint bank account, so my wages were paid straight into it—and he could see on the statement if I'd bought something on our debit card, or if I'd taken some money out. So I had to lie even more. I bought all my books second-hand, hid them round a friend's and told him I'd spent the money on...' She swallowed hard. 'On jewellery.'

'Oh, Alex.' No wonder she'd flinched when he'd mentioned jewellery. He squeezed her hand.

'And whenever he bought me jewellery...' She closed her eyes. 'There was always a reason. Not because he wanted to do something nice for me. Because he wanted to soften me up a bit. And he expected...'

Jordan was truly shocked at what she was implying. 'He *forced* you?'

'No. But he wanted a baby. He decided that we were going to start a family—he thought that would keep me too busy to think about my A levels and my career.'

Jordan remembered what she'd said last night about the ectopic pregnancy, how it made falling pregnant that bit more difficult, and he had a nasty feeling what was coming next. 'And you couldn't?'

She closed her eyes. 'Maybe if we'd had a baby, he would've been happy and we could've rubbed along better.'

'No,' he said gently. 'Having a baby wouldn't have papered over the cracks in your marriage. The cracks would've been made bigger by the sheer strain of broken nights and feeds and nappy changes, not to mention all the worries until you get used to being a parent.'

She looked at him. 'If you hadn't already told me you don't have children, that'd sound a bit personal.'

'Not me. One of my friends from university...he and his wife were having problems. They had a baby, thinking it would bring them closer together and save their marriage. That's when it got seriously messy.' He sighed. 'Lindsey did suggest it, but I remembered what had happened to Mark and said no.'

'I should've said no, too. Or at least told Nathan about our—' Her voice cracked. 'Our baby.'

'You didn't tell him?'

She shook her head. 'I couldn't. I was trying to block it out. I know it was unfair of me. I know I should've said something. But I couldn't.'

'And I'd guess he didn't make it easy for you.' He squeezed her hand. 'I wish I'd known the truth all those years ago, Alex. It would've been different. I wouldn't have been able to do anything about the ectopic pregnancy, but I could've spared you what you went through with Bennett. And I would've encouraged you to retake your exams, go on to do your degree.' He paused. 'Just so you know, a degree doesn't make any difference to your job now. You have the professional qualifications, the experience and the enthusiasm. They're what count. And we're damn lucky to have you.'

'Don't be too nice to me,' she said. 'Because I don't want to cry.'

'It's not weak to cry,' he said softly. 'And, just so you know, my shoulder will always be there for you. Always.'

'Thank you.'

Her voice was thready, and he could see her blinking back the tears. Tears he knew she didn't want to shed in public. He'd already pushed her far enough. 'Come on. Let's go and find somewhere to eat tonight.'

'St Mark's Square?' she suggested.

'Sounds great.'

They wandered into the square, looked at menus, and

booked dinner for two at one of the oldest *caffès* in Venice.
And then he took her to their hotel, so they could change.

She stopped dead outside the hotel and stared at him.
'Jordan, even I know that this is one of the most expensive
hotels in Venice. Everyone's heard of this place.'

He shrugged. 'And?'

'And...' She shook her head. 'Where do I begin?'

'What you do,' he said softly, 'is just enjoy it. I thought,
since we're playing hooky, we might as well do it in style.'

She still looked worried, and he sighed. He knew now
that Bennett had always had some kind of hidden agenda,
and it had stopped her enjoying things because she wondered what was going to be required of her in return. 'Alex.
You're with *me*. There aren't any hidden agendas. We're
having one night in Venice, and I just wanted it to be somewhere a bit special. Not because I expect something from
you, but because I want to make you feel like a princess.'

'Sorry. I don't mean to be ungrateful.' She gave him a
rueful smile. 'Thank you. It's lovely to be spoiled.'

'Let's go and find our room,' he said, taking her hand
and drawing her with him to the reception area.

When he opened the door to their suite, the first thing
he noticed was how huge the bed was. The bathroom was
pure marble with a large, deep bath, and there were exquisite antique glass chandeliers and mirrors everywhere.
Voile and silk curtains hung at the windows, and the bed
coverlets were also silk. The table and dressing table were
exquisite gilt ormolu, with Louis XIV chairs upholstered
in smoky blue velvet, while the carpet was definitely deep
enough to sink into as you walked.

'Wow. This is incredible.' She went over to one of the
windows, twitched the voile aside and exclaimed in delight. 'Jordan, we've got a view of the Grand Canal itself.
It's amazing.'

He stood behind her and wrapped his arms round her waist, resting his chin on her shoulder as he looked out at the view. 'Yes, it's really something.'

But the real thing for him was sharing this with her. The woman he loved.

And there were no two ways about it. He did love Alexandra. He'd loved her when he was nineteen, little more than a boy—and he still loved her now he was a man. It wasn't just the physical attraction; being with her made him feel different. With her, he could be himself and know that she understood him.

But did she feel the same way about him? Had Bennett damaged her so much that she'd never be able to love or trust someone again?

He kissed the nape of her neck. 'Alex?'

She shifted round to face him. 'We need to get ready.'

'So we do.' He gave her a wolfish grin, then scooped her up and carried her into the bathroom. She was about to protest, when he lowered his head and kissed her. And then everything went haywire.

She had no idea who took whose clothes off—everything was blurred by need and desire—but then they were both naked, both standing in the huge marble bath, and he'd turned the shower on so that warm water was spraying down over them.

'You're all tense.' He turned her so that her back was to him, and she felt him smooth shower gel over her shoulders. 'Here, and here.' He worked the knots out of her muscles, and she was surprised by how good it felt. Then he slid his hands round to her midriff, spreading his fingers, and drew her back against him. She could feel his erection pressing against her, and desire licked all the way down her spine. If only he'd move his hands up. Cup her breasts properly, ease the ache in her nipples.

'Your wish is my command,' he said softly against her ear, and she felt colour shoot through her face when she realised she'd spoken aloud.

'Sorry.'

He turned her to face him. 'For being demanding?' Amusement glittered in his eyes.

'I don't normally…'

'Well, you should.' He stole a kiss. 'I like it when you tell me what you want.' He poured more shower gel over her breasts, then stroked it into lather. 'Like this?'

She caught her breath as he teased her nipples into tight points. 'Yes.'

'Good.'

Here she was, need coiling tighter and tighter, to the point where she was almost begging him to take her now, finish it, because the tension was too much for her. And he was completely in control.

So not fair.

She wanted him in the same state that she was. Desperate.

It was time to take some of the control back. She grabbed the shower gel and smoothed some across his chest.

'Oh, now, that's nice. I like having your hands on me,' he said, his voice deepening.

He reminded her of a perfume ad, with his hair plastered back like that and his skin wet. Sexy as hell.

'How about here?' She let her hand drift lower, brushing over his abdomen—and it pleased her to note that he seemed to be having trouble breathing.

'Keep going, Alex.' His voice was deeper, too, slightly rougher with desire.

'You want me to touch you?' She curled her hand round his shaft. Stroked.

He closed his eyes and tipped his head back. 'Careful,' he warned. 'Carry on like this, and I'm not going to be much good to you.'

'Then perhaps I'd better stop.' She gave him her wickedest smile, and put her hands behind her back.

'That,' he said, 'is so...' He dragged in a breath. 'Alex. I need you. Now.'

'Now,' she agreed huskily.

It was a matter of seconds for him to step out of the shower, grab the wallet from his jeans and take a condom from it. It didn't seem to bother him that he was dripping water all over the floor and all over the tangle of their clothes—and it stopped bothering her, too, when he returned to the bath and lifted her up so that her back was against the tiles and the water was pouring over both of them. Automatically, she wrapped her legs round his waist for balance; and then he was pushing inside her, filling her, taking away the ache of frustration.

Her climax hit sooner than she'd expected; as her body tightened round his, he kissed her hard and she felt him shudder against her.

'I think,' he said shakily afterwards, 'we both needed that.'

'It feels as if I can breathe again.'

'Yeah.' He stroked her face. 'Come on. We'll look like prunes if we stay in here much longer.' He wrapped her in a fluffy towel and dried her.

And then she realised that half her clothes were soaked.

'Sorry, my fault,' he said. 'I was, um, thinking about other things.'

Like how quickly he could find a condom and be inside her. Yeah. That had been uppermost in her mind, too.

He looked at the mess on the floor. 'Just as well we bought clean stuff for tomorrow,' he said, but he was smiling. 'Could've been worse. I'll sort it out in a minute. Come on, we need to get changed or we'll be late for dinner.'

'I think,' she said, 'we'd better get changed in separate rooms.'

'Mmm, because you're too tempting.' He stole a kiss. 'Alex. You know the thing I'm most looking forward to, tonight? Falling asleep with you in my arms.'

So was she. Too much so. But she wasn't going to spoil tonight with worries. She was just going to let herself enjoy it. Store up the good memories. 'Go and get changed,' she said with a smile. 'I'll see you in a bit.'

CHAPTER ELEVEN

JORDAN took one look at Alexandra when she emerged from the bathroom, and his jaw dropped. 'Wow. That dress is gorgeous. And I can't wait to take it off you.'

She just laughed. 'Patience is a virtue. And a business asset.'

'I can be patient.' He pulled her into his arms and drew a line of kisses along the curve of her neck. 'I bet I can be more patient than you.'

'In your dreams.' She kissed him lightly. 'You don't scrub up so badly, yourself, Mr Smith. I like this shirt.' She skated her fingertips along the soft cotton. 'It brings out the colour of your eyes. Gorgeous.'

'The shirt, or my eyes?' he teased.

'Stop fishing.' But her eyes were glittering with amusement. 'Both.'

'Come on, we've got enough time for a walk before dinner.'

When they walked along the Grand Canal, a gondolier wearing the traditional black and white striped jersey and straw boater came over to them. 'Gondola, sir, madam, gondo-laaaa?' he asked hopefully.

'I guess if you're in Venice, you really have to take a ride in a gondola—it's something you can't do anywhere else,' Jordan said. 'Shall we?'

'That'd be nice.' But when Alexandra stepped in, the boat rocked wildly. 'Whoa,' she said, putting a hand out for balance.

Jordan stepped down beside her and steadied her. 'OK?'

'Yes. It just feels a bit—well—rickety,' she said in a whisper, not wanting to be rude to the gondolier.

He smiled. 'It's safe. Really. These boats have been sailing the canals of Venice for hundreds of years—well, obviously not this particular one, but boats just like it.'

She sat on the padded seat in front of where the gondolier stood. Jordan joined her, put his arm round her and drew her close.

As the gondolier poled them along the canal, she could see the sky fading from blue to rose pink at the horizon. Venus rose, shining almost as brightly as the moon; and then there were the first pinpoints of stars peeping through the velvety deep blue sky.

'Oh, wow, it's just…' Words failed her. This was like nothing else she'd ever experienced. Romantic didn't even begin to cover it.

And she was so glad that she was sharing this with him.

As the boat glided silently under a bridge, Jordan kissed her, his mouth warm and soft and sweet and tender; it started out reassuring, but she could feel the tension in his body, telling her that he was trying to hold back.

But the narrow little canals they were gliding through weren't lit by streetlamps, like the main thoroughfares; there was just the occasional glow from a window. Meaning that this was much, much more private than either of them had expected—just them and the starlight. And so, under the next bridge, she kissed him, nipping gently at his lower lip until he let her deepen the kiss.

God, she loved kissing him. The way he responded to her. The way he made her respond to him. The way her blood felt as if it were fizzing through her veins. He made her feel as if she had a permanent fever.

He broke the kiss as light started to draw nearer; as they reached the end of the canal, Alexandra realised what it was. The Grand Canal, its ancient buildings spot lit against the night. She glanced at Jordan; his mouth was slightly swollen from kissing her, and it was a fair bet she was in the same state. But she just hadn't been able to stop herself. 'Sorry,' she muttered.

'I'm not,' Jordan whispered in her ear. And then he gave her an incredibly wicked, sensual smile that made her feel a hell of a lot better. It hadn't just been her.

Eventually the gondola stopped by the Rialto Bridge; the gondolier helped them both out and wished them a nice evening. Hand in hand, they wandered back to St Mark's Square. The piazza was all lit up with huge round lanterns in the lower arches of the arcades and smaller ones in the two upper layers. String quartets and pianists performed in pergolas outside the *caffés*, filling the square with soft jazz and gentle classical music. Some people were sitting outside at the tables, listening to the music and sipping wine; couples walked through the square with their arms wrapped round each other; and others were actually dancing through the square.

'We have to do it,' Jordan said. 'Especially to this song.'

One of the quartets was playing 'It Had to Be You' and the vocalist had a smoky, sexy voice. Jordan spun her into his arms and danced with her through the square, spinning her round.

'I had no idea you could do ballroom dancing,' she said.

'I don't exactly advertise it,' he said with a grin. 'And this, my sweet Alexandra, is a foxtrot we're doing, I'll have you know.'

'A foxtrot?' She didn't have a clue how to do a foxtrot—she'd never done any kind of ballroom dancing—but Jordan led her so well that dancing with him was effortless. And fun. To the point where she didn't mind the fact that he was in control, because she knew he wasn't going to hurt her the way that Nathan had. And she loved the fact that he was singing the song to her—even the bit accusing her of being bossy. Which she could be. He'd never sung to her before, so she'd had no idea that his voice was so nice: a warm, soulful tenor.

'I would've made you sing "O Sole Mio" on the gondola, if I'd known you were this good,' she teased.

'Ah, so the lady would like to be serenaded? It can be arranged,' he teased back. 'But first…' He bent her back over his arm and kissed her. Thoroughly. She was flushed and laughing when they straightened up again.

'Dinner,' he said, still holding her gaze.

She was still smiling when they finally walked through the door of the *caffè* to claim their table in the restaurant.

'Today has been amazing,' she said softly, 'just amazing. This is everything I always thought Venice would be, and more. Thank you so much.'

'My pleasure. And I mean that. I'm glad I'm sharing it with you,' Jordan said.

The food was perfectly cooked, a riot of textures and flavours. But Alexandra especially liked the Venetian cookies that came with their coffee: thin slices of almond sponge, the layers coloured delicately green, red and white like the Italian flag, wrapped in melted chocolate. 'I'm going to talk Giorgio into making some of these for us when we get back to London.'

'Mmm. And I'm going to feed them to you bite by bite.' His gaze held hers. 'In bed.'

Her pulse rate kicked up a notch. 'I think I'm done with coffee.' All she wanted was him. Naked. Beneath her.

'Me, too.' He moistened his lower lip with his tongue. 'We need to get out of here.'

He wrapped his arm round her shoulder as they left the *caffè*, and she slid hers round his waist; he shortened his stride to match hers, and they got back to their hotel in record time.

'I rushed you back here,' he said in the reception area. 'And it's not even late. I should've taken you out for Bellinis.' The mixture of sparkling wine and puréed peach was one of the most famous cocktails in the world. 'Except right now I don't want to have to share you with anyone else.'

She knew exactly what he meant. She just wanted to be with him, too. It wasn't the same kind of possessiveness that Nathan had shown; it felt different. And she knew that Jordan wouldn't try to choose her friends and put barriers between her and the people who knew her best.

'So what do you suggest?'

'The balcony in our room. Bellinis, watching the night. And…' He didn't say the rest of it, but she knew exactly what he had in mind, and her body tingled with anticipation.

'Yes,' she said huskily.

He ordered their drinks at the bar, then came back over to her. 'Room Service is bringing them up,' he said. 'Let's go.'

Though when he opened the French windows and they stepped out onto the balcony, they discovered that it was a little cooler than they'd both expected.

The sky had darkened while they'd been eating and the waters of the lagoon had turned from turquoise to inky black, reflecting the lights from the building; the churches were lit from below, making them seem almost ghostly. And all around was silent, the soft lapping of the tide—

no noisy engines or roaring exhausts. She loved seeing
the Thames lit up at night, but that paled into comparison
with this, with the reflections of the lights on the lagoon
and the occasional gondola or night *vaporetto* going past.
The whole scene before them was just magical.

'Are you cold?' he asked.

'I'm fine,' she fibbed.

Though clearly he noticed the goose-pimples on her
arms, because he smiled and wrapped his arms round her,
drawing her back against his body. 'Time to share some
bodily warmth, I think.'

She relaxed against him, her head against his shoulder, and his hands splayed across her midriff. His thumbs
brushed the undersides of her breasts through her dress,
and the thought of what he was going to do next made her
nipples harden.

Slowly, softly, he moved so that he was cupping her
breasts. She closed her eyes as his thumbs circled her nipples, teasing them; and then she felt his mouth against the
curve of her neck, making her arch back against him.

Just as she was about to turn round, kiss him and walk
him backwards into their room, there was a knock at the
door.

He groaned. 'Bad timing. Room service. I'll get it,' he
said. 'Stay here.'

He returned carrying two Bellinis in champagne flutes,
each decorated with a single strawberry.

'To us,' he said softly, raising his glass. 'And to tonight.'

'To us,' she echoed, raising her own glass, then took a
sip. She'd expected the cocktail to be a little over-sweet, but
the dryness of the sparkling wine cut through the sweetness of the fruit and gave the drink depth. 'This is gorgeous.'

He kissed her. 'And so are you.' He took her glass and

placed it on the coffee table next to his. 'I'm really glad that your dress doesn't have a tight skirt.'

'Why?' She wasn't following this. At all.

He walked her back out to the balcony and spun her round so that she was facing the Grand Canal. 'Because, even though I'm pretty sure we can't be seen from here...' And then she realised what he was doing. Slowly, gradually, tugging the hem of her dress up to her waist.

Adrenalin kicked through her. She'd never, ever done anything like this before. He was going to make love to her on the balcony overlooking the city? 'Jordan, we can't.'

'Yes, we can.' He kissed the nape of her neck, and then stroked one hand down to her thighs. 'Stockings?' His fingers found the lacy edge of her hold-ups and he exhaled harshly. 'If I'd known about this, we wouldn't have made it to dinner. And I might just've had to find a deserted *calle.*'

'And got us both arrested. Jordan, if someone looks up—'

'They'll see you, looking out over the lagoon. They'll see me standing behind you. And this balcony is waist-high.'

'Wrought iron.'

'Covered in plants. The perfect screen.' He nibbled her earlobe. 'Neither of us is a screamer. Nobody's going to know. Just you and me.'

Making love on the balcony of the poshest hotel in Venice. He had to be crazy.

His hands were spread across her midriff again, and he'd moved so she could feel his erection pressing against her. Her mouth went dry. 'Jordan. Yes.'

It took him seconds to protect them both. 'Hold on to the balcony rail,' he directed.

She did so, and he positioned himself at her entrance, then slowly pushed inside her.

'Oh, my God,' she breathed.

'Good?' he asked softly.

'Yeah. Unbelievable.'

'Keep watching the lagoon,' he said.

Though she couldn't. As the tension built and built and built inside her, she squeezed her eyes shut and tipped her head back. And then wave after wave of sensation rippled through her as she hit her climax.

He was careful with her afterwards, walking backwards into their room and drawing her with him, and then closing the French doors. And then he carried her to their bed and undressed her achingly slowly, caressing every centimetre of skin he revealed before making love with her again.

As her pulse slowed and he drew her into his arms, cuddled against her, she actually found herself crying.

Jordan kissed her tears away. 'Don't cry, Alex,' he urged softly.

'They're happy tears,' she said. 'I promise.'

Though there was a hint of sadness, too. How she wished that the past couldn't cast its blight on her future.

She was going to have to tell him the truth. But not yet. She wanted to have tonight and tomorrow morning. Such precious memories.

She fell asleep in his arms, thinking, *I love you. If only there was a way for us to make this work.*

The next morning, Jordan woke first. He lay there for a while, just watching Alexandra sleep; the wariness had gone from her face, and in repose she was beautiful.

Funny, before, he'd been so sure that his life had direction and purpose and meaning. But, now that Alexandra was back in his life, he realised just how much he'd been kidding himself. He'd been working silly hours to distract himself from the fact that his life was empty and he envied the hell out of his best friend and his wife, who were so much in love with each other and were expecting their first child.

He could imagine Alexandra like that, radiant in pregnancy, her belly rounded by their child, and the thought made his head spin. Alexandra and their baby. A family. The family that they'd so nearly made all those years ago.

He kissed her awake, and she smiled at him.

'Hello.' Her brown eyes were all soft and warm, and for a moment Jordan was sure that they were full of love.

Then the wariness came back. He could even see it happening, and sighed inwardly. She'd told him more about her past, she'd let him close enough to actually spend the night with him—but he could tell that there were still more barriers. More things she hadn't told him.

Would he ever be able to teach her to trust again?

'Good morning.' He kissed her gently. 'Shall I order room service or, since the sun's shining, shall we go and have breakfast on the terrace? Apparently, the views are stunning.'

'We could have room service absolutely anywhere,' she said. 'But breakfast on the Grand Canal... That's a once-in-a-lifetime thing.' Her smile was bright—and, to his relief, genuine. 'I think we have to do it, Jordan.'

The terrace had amazing views over the lagoon, and the sun was so warm that Alexandra could barely believe it was only April. She enjoyed every second of it, from the ruby-red freshly squeezed orange juice to the plate of warm pastries to the huge silver pot of coffee. 'This,' she said,

leaning back in her chair, 'is what I call being pampered.
And it's wonderful.'

'Good. Our flight isn't until this afternoon, so we still
have a bit of time to go exploring. Would you like to go
over to Murano and see the glass being made?' Jordan
asked.

'That'd be lovely.'

When they'd finished their coffee, they headed out to
the Grand Canal and took the *vaporetto* over to Murano.
They were both entranced by the glass blowers and how
quickly they could turn a ball of orangey-yellow glass into
a rearing horse with a windblown mane and tail—and then
how a similar ball of glass could be blown into the most
beautiful vase.

After the demonstration, they wandered through the
glass warehouses. Alexandra noticed Jordan picking up
a paperweight for a closer inspection; the expression on
his face told her he loved it, but for some reason he put it
down again.

She sneaked a glance at the glass; it was the same colour as the bowl she'd sighed over in Venice and the starfish pendant he'd bought her. She managed to distract him,
then bought it swiftly, and had it wrapped and hidden in
her bag before he could notice anything had happened.

They stopped off in Burano on the way back; Alexandra
loved the pretty painted houses and took photographs of
the buildings' reflections in the canals. They wandered
through the main street, looking at the lace, and stopped
to buy some of the lemony S-shaped biscuits the island
was famous for.

And on the way back to their hotel on the *vaporetto*,
she handed him the beautifully wrapped parcel.

'What's this?' he asked.

'For you.'

He frowned. 'You don't have buy me anything.'

She shrugged and threw his words back at him. 'I'm your girlfriend. I'm allowed to buy you something if I want to.' She softened the words with a smile.

'Thank you.' He opened the parcel and sucked in a breath. 'Alex, that's gorgeous. How did you know that was the one I had my eye on?'

Because she'd been watching him. Not that she was going to tell him that. 'Lucky guess,' she fibbed.

'It's gorgeous,' he said again. 'Thank you.' He kissed her lightly.

Back at the hotel, they prepared to leave for London. Their clothes from the day before were still slightly damp from their soaking in the bathroom, but he shoved them all into the case anyway.

Alexandra started laughing.

He looked at her. 'What's so funny?'

'I can't believe someone as pernickety as you packs like that.'

'It's all going straight into the washing machine or the dry cleaner's when we get back to London, so what's the point of packing neatly?'

'I guess you have a point.'

At the airport, she was relieved to discover that that their case was indeed small enough to count as hand luggage. Jordan held her hand all the way back to London, except this wasn't like coming to Venice, when she'd been so thrilled at the idea of finally visiting the place that had been top of her wish list. Now, they were going back to reality, things that couldn't be escaped. And she was going to have to tell him the rest of it.

Dread settled into a hard knot in her stomach when they landed, and her feet felt as if they were dragging as they went through Customs.

Outside the airport, Jordan hailed a taxi and gave the driver her address.

'We need to sort out our luggage,' she said as the taxi driver pulled up outside her flat. 'Do you want to come in for a bit?'

'Thanks. That'd be nice.'

Home. Except it never really had been, she thought as she opened the front door. It had been just a place to live. Somewhere to cook, somewhere to sleep. Whereas Venice—Venice had felt like home. And she knew why. Because she'd been with Jordan all the time. She'd fallen asleep in his arms, been woken by him in the morning with a kiss…

What an idiot she was.

'Penny for them?' he asked.

She shook herself. 'Just that London feels a bit cold and flat, after Venice.'

'Yeah. I know what you mean. Though I guess, to a Venetian, London would seem exotic. All the green spaces and gardens we have instead of courtyards and jetties and bridges.'

'I'd better sort out the case.' She opened it in front of her washing machine, then paused and looked up at him. 'You know, I might as well put your stuff in with mine.'

This was the opening Jordan had hoped for. A chance to move another step closer. 'And I'll collect them tomorrow night? Thanks. That'd be good.' He waited a beat. 'Or I could keep them here. As spare clothes. Just as you could keep some things at mine.'

She said nothing, but went very still.

Oh, hell. He'd taken it too far, pushed her too fast. 'It was just an idea,' he said lightly.

'Mmm,' she said, and started putting the laundry straight into the washing machine.

And now he felt completely awkward. 'Shall I make some coffee, or something?'

'As you wish.'

Hell, hell, hell. That offhand tone was deliberate, he was sure. She was putting every single barrier back into place.

There was only one thing he could think of to do to stop her. He dropped to his knees beside her. 'Alex.'

She looked up. 'Yes?'

He dipped his head. Brushed his mouth oh, so lightly against hers. His lips tingled, and he did it again. And again, until her arms were wrapped round his neck and she was kissing him back, opening her mouth to let him deepen the kiss. His pulse was hammering so hard, he could practically hear it, and his temperature had gone up several degrees.

'Forget the washing,' he said, pulling her to her feet, then scooped her up and carried her to her bedroom.

'Jordan, sex isn't the answer to everything,' she protested as he set her back down on her feet.

'No, but I can't think of any other way to stop you putting the barriers back up between us.' He stroked her face. 'Last night, I fell asleep with you in my arms. This morning, you were the first thing I saw when I woke. And I don't want last night to be a one-off.'

She sucked in a breath. 'So what exactly do you want?'

'You,' he said. 'I know I'm rushing you. I'm trying not to. But this weekend's been so special to me. I don't want to go back to how things were, having to leave you in bed and going home to a cold, empty flat.' He stole another kiss. 'It's too soon to move in together. I know that. I'm not asking for that.' Not yet. 'But I'd like to be able to stay

over, and for you to stay at my place. Not every night—
just sometimes.' He stole another kiss. 'Preferably starting tonight.'

'You want to stay tonight.' It was a statement, not a
question.

'Which isn't a string attached to Venice.' He sighed.
'It's got nothing to do with Venice at all. Well, I suppose
it has.' He stroked her face. 'I enjoyed waking up with
you and it's made me realise how much I want to do that
again.'

She bit her lip, looking worried.

'Let's keep it simple,' he said softly. 'I like being with
you, and I think you like being with me.'

She nodded.

'So can I stay tonight?' When she said nothing, he
added, 'I don't want you to say yes because you feel any
obligation to me for Venice. I want you to say yes because
you want me to stay. Because you want to fall asleep in
my arms. Because you want to wake up with me tomorrow, just as I want to wake up with you.'

For a moment, her eyes glittered with tears.

And then she whispered, 'Yes.'

CHAPTER TWELVE

WITHIN a week Jordan had a shelf in Alexandra's bathroom and space in her wardrobe, and she had the same at his flat. What she'd promised herself would just be an occasional night spent together turned out to be every night, because now they'd actually slept together and woken up together, they discovered that they just couldn't bear to be apart.

And every day Alexandra realised she was falling more and more in love with Jordan.

She was going to have to talk to him. Tell him the bit she'd kept back. The longer she left it, the harder she knew it was going to be—for both of them.

She left work early on the Friday night; the plan was that Jordan was coming over for dinner and to watch a movie when he'd finished at the office. He texted her to let her know that he was on his way; when he arrived, he kissed her lingeringly. 'OK?'

No. She was very far from OK. But she forced a smile to her face. 'Sure. Just a bit tired.'

It felt like the last meal of the condemned prisoner; her stomach was in a knot, and she couldn't eat. She toyed with her food. Eventually Jordan laid down his cutlery, his own meal only half-eaten, and reached over to take her hand. 'What's wrong?'

Where did she start?

'We need to talk,' she said.

'I had a feeling you were going to say that. You've been antsy for a week.' He squeezed her hand. 'Tell me,' he said softly.

'It's about Nathan.'

'He's been in touch with you?'

She shook her head. 'It's about the reason why my marriage broke up.'

He frowned. 'I thought that was because he was a total control freak who bullied you, kept you apart from your friends and your family, and tried to push you into what he wanted to do regardless of what you wanted.'

'That was part of it,' she said, 'but I can't let him take all the blame. Part of it was me. I let him down.'

'How?' He looked puzzled. 'Because you wouldn't let him use you as a doormat?'

'No. I couldn't give him a child.' She dragged in a breath. 'Our baby...it wasn't the only one I lost. I lost Nathan's, too. Except I didn't realise I was pregnant at the time.' Every word felt as if she were cutting into the scars. But she knew it had to be done. She had to be honest. Tell Jordan the whole story, so he knew what he was getting in to if he stayed with her. To give him the option to leave. 'I had what I thought was just a really light period. And then, two weeks later, I collapsed at work.' She shivered. 'I knew what that pain meant. I'd been there before. And I didn't get to the hospital in time. I lost the baby and they couldn't save the other tube.'

She lifted her chin, aiming for defiance, but then the whole thing was undermined because she had to blink back the tears. 'That's what you need to know. I can't have a baby now. Not unless I do it through IVF.' She closed her eyes. 'And, after two ectopic pregnancies, I just can't face that.'

He released her hand. Just as Alexandra had expected: he couldn't handle this any more than Nathan had been able to. She couldn't look at him; she couldn't bear to see the mingled pity and disappointment in his face.

But when she felt herself being scooped out of her chair, she opened her eyes again. 'What are you doing?'

'This is a conversation where I think you need to be held,' Jordan said, sitting down in her chair and settling her on his lap. 'So that's what I'm doing. Holding you.'

'Didn't you hear what I just said? I can't have a baby.'

'And?'

How could he sound so casual? 'But—don't you want children?' She frowned. 'Don't you need a child, an heir for Field's?'

'Not necessarily.'

'But Nathan…'

'I'm not Nathan.' He looked hurt. 'Alex, the last few weeks—I thought we'd got closer.'

'We have. Which is why we need to have this conversation now. So I can let you go, and you can find someone who'll give you the child you need.' Her voice was thick with tears. 'I'll be handing in my resignation, first thing Monday morning.'

Jordan could barely believe what he was hearing. She was walking out on him and she was going to leave Field's? 'Why?'

'I can't stay at Field's any more. I can't work with you, Jordan.'

He frowned. 'I'm missing something here.' They'd developed a good working relationship. They were a team. 'Why can't you work with me?'

Her breath hitched. 'Because I'm not nice enough to be

able to stand by and smile and be pleased for you when you find someone else.'

What? Where was this all coming from? 'I'm not going to find someone else.'

'Of course you are. You just have to smile at women and they melt.'

'That's crazy. Of course they don't. And, more importantly, I don't want anyone else.' He sighed. 'Alex, it's you. It's always been you—even when I thought I hated you. I never loved Lindsey, and I guess that's the real reason why my marriage didn't work. She wasn't you. I should never have asked her to marry me.'

Alexandra looked anguished. 'But I can't give you an heir for Field's, Jordan. I can't conceive without IVF, and besides there are no guarantees that IVF will work.' She bit her lip. 'And I can't live with the guilt and the strain of another failure. I just can't.'

'You don't have to,' he said softly. 'I'm not Nathan. I'm not going to make you go through something you don't want to do.' He paused. 'So I take it he didn't support you when you lost the baby?'

She swallowed hard. 'He said I'd lied to him. Lied by omission. Which was true—I should've told him about our baby. I should've been more careful. I should've taken a pregnancy test anyway, because my period was lighter than normal and I should've realised there was a chance I might be pregnant.'

How had the man managed to make her feel that everything was her fault? Why hadn't he shown the slightest bit of sympathy? Why hadn't he put her needs first, at a time when she'd been at her most vulnerable? 'Don't blame yourself,' Jordan said fiercely. 'The way I see it, he should never have pushed you like that. You were only eighteen when you married him, you'd already had a really rough time without the support you needed from me or your parents, and he should've talked to you and found out how you felt about starting a family. And then he should've waited until you were ready instead of pressuring you.'

'I thought he would wait,' she whispered. 'That first year, when he was so good to me—I actually thought I could be happy. And then it changed. After the fight about my exams…we didn't make love any more. It was just sex, to make babies. We only ever had sex when it was the right time of the month, the time when I was most likely to conceive. And I felt he wasn't seeing me any more; all he saw was someone who could give him a child.'

'Why didn't you leave him?'

'Because I'd lost myself,' she said. 'Day by day, I'd let him take over more and more. When it's gradual like that, you don't realise how bad things are getting until you're right at rock bottom. And I'm so ashamed that I let someone control me that way.' Her breath shuddered. 'I deferred to him in everything. I hate it that I was so weak, so pathetic.'

'You weren't pathetic. You were young. And when you stopped letting him make all the decisions—when you'd finally started to get over how I let you down and wanted to do things for yourself, retake your exams and get on with your life—he couldn't handle it. So it was his problem, not yours,' Jordan said.

'It didn't feel like it,' she said. 'I felt as if I was the selfish one. He'd done so much for me, he'd given me a home and a future; and I wouldn't even give him the one thing he wanted, a baby. I tried to tell him about you, about what happened to our baby. But every time I tried, I saw the way he looked at me—he despised me, Jordan.'

'You're worth a million of him. And he was the one with

the problem, not you,' Jordan repeated. 'Couldn't you have
told Meggie what was going on? Your parents?'

'I hardly saw my parents. I—' How could she explain?
'We grew apart, after I left home. Nathan didn't try to build
any bridges with my parents because he said I didn't need
anyone else except my husband. And Meggie…he didn't
like her.' She bit her lip. 'In the end, I could only see her
at lunchtime, and even then I had to make up an excuse
about where I'd been.'

'I'd like to break every bone in his body—twice,' Jordan
said.

Then he saw the fear in her eyes.

She'd said that Bennett hadn't hit her. Maybe she hadn't
told him the whole truth about that, either. Wasn't that how
bullies worked, making their victims feel as if it was their
fault and they were completely worthless?

'But I wouldn't do that,' he said, trying to make his
voice gentle, 'because violence doesn't solve anything.
And what he really needs is professional help, because the
way he treated you wasn't normal. That isn't how an equal
relationship works, Alex.'

'He couldn't forgive me,' she said, 'for not giving him a
child. For not being a proper wife. He went on and on and
on about IVF. How, if I really loved him, I'd book myself
in to a clinic and start treatment.'

'And if he'd really loved you,' Jordan said dryly, 'he
wouldn't have asked you to do that. He would've realised
that you'd been through more than enough. If you'd wanted
to do it, if you'd been desperate for a child of your own,
then fine. But it's not an easy procedure. And, like you
said, there are no guarantees it'll work.'

'That's not how Nathan saw it. He went on and on and
on about it. It was only one of my clients that kept me sane.'

'Clients?' Jordan asked.

'Didn't you read my CV when you interviewed me? I was a cleaner for three years.'

'I don't remember seeing anything like that on your CV.'

'The agency probably put a spin on it and called it domestic client management or something. I worked for a domestic agency when I left home. It meant doing a bit of cleaning, doing their shopping, and maybe making them a sandwich or heating through some kind of ready meal.'

A job that needed no academic qualifications. And Alexandra had been so academic. Why hadn't she held out for a job that would stretch her more?

As if the question showed on his face, she said softly, 'Jordan, I needed to earn a living and I'd failed my A levels, remember. My savings weren't that huge, so I wasn't in a position to be fussy. And actually, I liked my job. I liked meeting different people and making a difference to their lives.'

Now that he could understand. Because the Alexandra he remembered—the Alexandra he'd got to know again—had always been kind, making the effort to help people. 'So you had a nice client?'

'I had several nice clients, but Jude was the best. She used to be an actress. She had this parrot, Jasper, who used to quote Shakespeare. She'd gone through several lots of domestic help because they were terrified of him—he used to sit on your shoulder, say, "No bitey", and then nip your earlobe. And sometimes he'd land on your head, just to freak you. But he made friends with me, and I loved it when he sang a little song or quoted Shakespeare.' She smiled at the memory. 'And one day I forgot myself and spoke the next few lines of the play he'd been quoting.'

He could imagine that. It was a game they'd played so

many times themselves, when he'd been helping her study. He'd rewarded her with kisses when she got it right.

'Jude heard me. She made me sit down with her over a cup of tea and tell her how come I could quote from the middle of *The Winter's Tale*. Eventually I told her the whole story. And she made me see that I wasn't doing everything I could with my life. And my friend who'd been taking the classes with me…she said the same thing. She was the one who made me do the career tests. To see that I was worth more than Nathan let me think I was.'

'You're worth a hell of a lot more,' he said.

'It didn't feel like it at the time. It felt like yet another in a long line of failures. He wanted a baby; I couldn't give him one. I was a failure as a wife, a failure as a mother—everything I touched, I failed.' She dragged in a breath. 'I didn't tell him I was doing my exams. I made excuses, told more lies. I took the exams. And then I got my results.'

'Top marks.' Even if Jordan hadn't seen her CV, he would've known that.

'I knew I wasn't going to university, but it made me think that maybe I could still do exams. Maybe I could do some kind of vocational or professional qualification.'

'Like the marketing exams.'

'The ones my friend suggested.' She nodded. 'When I told Nathan I was going to change my job and do my professional qualifications, he said I couldn't study and have a family. I told him there was no way I was going through IVF. After two ectopic pregnancies, all that pain and all that loss, I couldn't face it. Month after month of having to inject myself with hormones and then going through all the procedures, hoping that they could collect enough eggs and fertilise them, that a viable embryo could be put back and then…' She swallowed hard. 'I'd already lost two babies, and there's only a one in four chance that IVF will work. Every cycle that didn't work would've brought that back to me, and I just couldn't handle it.'

Jordan held her closer. 'Of course you couldn't.'

'Things got worse and worse between us. He said I was a failure as a wife, a total failure. And he was going to divorce me for unreasonable behaviour.'

'What? But he was the one being unreasonable.'

'I waited until he'd gone to work, one morning, then packed my stuff and walked out. I left him a letter saying I was sorry, I couldn't stay married to him any more so I was leaving, so he could find someone who'd give him what he wanted.'

The same kind of thing she'd just said to him, Jordan thought. Except what he and Bennett wanted were very, very different things.

And she clearly hadn't finished, because she was shaking. He stroked her hair, hoping that it would give her the strength to go on. To tell him the rest, and let him help her wipe the rest of the shadows out of her life.

'He waited for me outside the office, knowing I'd have to go there to give in my time sheet, and he told me that I had to come back to him. I said no. My boss heard all the shouting and came out. He called the police. Nathan threatened to hit him. And it just got messy.' She blew out a breath. 'He ended up being taken into custody. I got an injunction so he couldn't come anywhere near me, before or after the divorce. And I swore I'd never let myself get in that position again. I'd never let my happiness rely on someone else. I never let anyone control me again.'

'I can understand that.' He held her close. There was one really important question he needed to ask. 'Do you know your own worth now?'

'Yes.'

'I'm glad.'

She looked miserable. 'It took me a lot of hard work to get to that point. And a fair bit of nagging from Meggie, Jude and Amy—my friend who suggested doing the marketing exams.'

'That's what friends are for,' he said lightly. And thank God she'd had some people to fight her corner when she needed it. 'Just for the record,' he said, 'I think you're bright—you have great ideas and they're grounded in reality. I think you're brave, because you've gone through hell in the last ten years and you don't whine about it to anyone, you just get on with things. I respect your judgement. And, most of all, I love you.' He stroked her face. 'Which isn't me pressuring you to love me back. I just don't want you to be in any doubt about how I feel about you.'

'You love me?' she asked in seeming wonder. 'Even after everything I've just told you?'

'I love you,' he repeated. He stole a kiss. 'I fell in love with you when you were a geeky seventeen-year-old. I loved everything about you. Your mind, your smile, your body. And it never really changed, even when I was angry with you, when I didn't know the truth about what was happening. Then, when we started working together, it drove me crazy—my common sense told me that I should keep you at a distance, but all I wanted to do was kiss you.' He smiled at her. 'Of all the department stores in all the towns in all the world, you walk into mine.'

She grimaced. 'That's the worst Bogart impersonation I've ever heard—and I hate that film anyway.'

'Ilsa walks off and sacrifices everything she had with Rick. Is that what you're going to do with me?'

She blew out a breath. 'Right now, I can't think straight—I can't make a sensible decision about anything.'

'Then don't make a decision now,' he said gently. 'And

please don't think that any of what you've just told me changes a single thing between us.'

'But—you need someone who can give you children.'

'We've already been through that, Alex. The way I see it, you've been through hell and more than enough pain. I'm not Bennett. I'm not going to make you go through a lot of painful, intrusive medical procedures just to boost my ego. If you want children, then there are other ways. We can adopt. We could foster. We could look into surrogacy. Or we could even not have children at all. We'll still be happy together.'

She blinked. 'What about Field's?'

'We can work something out. But I know what I need. I know what I want. And she's right here in my arms.'

She stroked his face. 'I wish I could believe that. But how do you know you're not going to regret that decision? Maybe not today. Maybe not tomorrow, but soon and—'

He stopped her protest by kissing her. 'For someone who says she hates *Casablanca*, you know an awful lot of the lines.'

'It was one of Nathan's favourites,' she said drily. 'One of the things we had in common—we both liked classic films. But I came to hate that one. The way Ilsa was trapped. Whatever she did, she lost. And I felt like that, too. Even though I wasn't seeing anyone else and neither was he.'

'Trapped between your marriage and your career.' That wasn't a mistake he was planning to make. As far as he was concerned, there was no reason why she couldn't have both. He'd back her, whatever she wanted to do. 'I'm sorry he didn't listen to you and let you do what you needed. But please don't think that all men are the same.'

'I know they're not,' she said dryly.

'And I want you to promise me something. If I say or

do anything in the future that makes you unhappy, challenge me. It might be crossed wires, or I might be being an idiot. But as long as we keep talking, we'll work it out. Together.'

'I'm not used to spilling my fears,' she said.

'I understand that. The important thing is that we'll listen to each other. Or try to—neither of us is perfect.'

'You're telling me.'

'I love you,' he said softly.

She held him close. 'I love you, too.' She took a deep breath. 'But if I'm honest, I'm really scared that I can't give you what you want. That I won't be enough for you.'

'All I want is you,' he said. 'You're enough for me. And I'm going to tell you that every single day, until you finally believe me.'

He could still see the wariness in her eyes. She wanted to believe him, but she couldn't make that step. Not yet.

Well, it wasn't going to happen instantly. She just needed to learn to trust him—and he knew that would take time.

The following weekend, Jordan came back from the office to find Alexandra brooding. Outwardly, she was simply brainstorming a project at her kitchen table; but he could see how spiky her handwriting was, how firm the strokes were. Something was bugging her. And the only way he'd find out what was by asking her directly.

'What's wrong?' he asked.

'Nothing. Just thinking about something,' she said.

'It's not nothing, or you'd look me in the eye.'

She sighed. 'OK. I talked to my parents this morning.' She bit her lip. 'I owe you an apology. Dad didn't ring you from the hospital. He—' her voice caught '—he said you'd already hurt me enough, and he thought it was better just to draw a line under the whole thing and not have you making it worse and dragging things out.'

And now she was wondering what would've happened if her father had phoned him. If things would've been different.

Jordan put his arms round her. 'Remember, we can't change the past. Just forgive it.'

'Mmm.' She really didn't sound in a forgiving mood.

'Want to know what I think? He was doing his best to protect you. He did what he thought was right at the time.' He kissed her. 'OK, he got it wrong, but he didn't do it out of malice. He did it out of love.'

She sighed. 'I guess so.'

'You used to be close to your parents,' he said softly. 'And I think you miss that. My guess is that they miss you, too, but they don't have a clue how to make things right between you—and they're scared of getting things even more wrong and making the rift wider.'

'So what are you saying?'

He scooped her up and sat down, settling her on his lap. 'Nobody's perfect. Maybe we need to start building bridges. Give everyone a chance to put their mistakes behind them. I know my mum's desperate to make it up with you, and I'd guess your parents are just as desperate.'

'So I need to make the first move?'

'We do,' he corrected gently. 'You're not on your own any more, Alex. I'm with you, every step of the way. Let's get rid of the bad stuff and make room for the good.' He kissed her again. 'I'm not saying you should do it right this minute. Just don't leave it to fester and hurt you.'

She sighed. 'You're right. I'll call them. We'll start building those bridges.'

'And that's another thing I love about you,' he said softly. 'Your bravery.'

'I'm not brave,' she said.

'You are in my eyes. And I love you.' He smiled at her. 'Always.'

Over the next month, Jordan told Alexandra that he loved her in every possible way. With a single red rose delivered to her desk. With a handwritten copy of a Shakespearean sonnet on marbled paper. With the CD of a song that had really appropriate words. With chocolate, hand-iced with the message JS ♥ AB. He stopped just short of hiring a sky-writer, knowing that she'd have a tart comment to make about environmental damage; but every day he found a different way to tell her that he loved her.

And every night, he told her in words; just before she fell asleep in his arms, he whispered, 'Alex, I love you. Always.'

As the days went past, the look of disbelief in her eyes that she always quickly tried to hide gradually started to fade. Until one day it wasn't there any more. She just smiled back at him. 'I love you, too.'

Tonight might just be the night, he thought, curling his fingers round the velvet-covered box he'd had for a week.

And he just hoped she'd listen to what he had to say.

A quick phone call ensured that his plans were work-able—at least from a logistics point of view. Now he had to convince Alexandra; and he knew that would be the hardest part.

He sent her an email.

Taking you out straight from work tonight. Can you be ready at half seven?

Two minutes later, she knocked on his office door. 'Where are we going?'

He spread his hands. 'I can't tell you.'

'Why not?'

'It's a surprise. One you'll like,' he added hastily. Or at least one he hoped she'd like.

'Can you at least tell me the dress code?'

'You're perfect as you are.' He blew her a kiss from his desk. 'Now go away and stop distracting me.'

'Yes, sir.' She gave him an insolent little salute.

He grinned, and waited until she was halfway out of the door before saying, 'Alex?'

She looked over her shoulder. 'Yes?'

'I love you.'

She smiled back. 'I love you, too.'

And hope bloomed in his heart.

The taxi was there dead on seven thirty, and Jordan refused to be drawn about where they we going. Until they rounded the corner and could see the London Eye, all lit up.

'Jordan?'

'It's the last ride of the night,' he said. 'And we have a ticket. I thought it might be fun.' Even though he managed to keep his tone relatively cool, his heart was hammering. *Please, please, let her say yes.*

'Do you know, I've never actually been on the London Eye?' She reached up to kiss him. 'This is a really lovely surprise, Jordan.'

This wasn't actually the surprise, he thought. And he had absolutely no idea how she was going to take this. It wasn't like an exam or a business deal, where he always had a pretty good idea how things were going. He just had to hope he'd got this right.

They went to the priority gate into the capsule. There was only one other person there.

She frowned. 'Jordan, shouldn't there be more people getting on?'

'No. It's a private capsule. Apart from the host being

there—' very discreetly in the background '—to keep the health and safety people happy, it's just us.'

And a bottle of champagne and two glasses. Which he really, really hoped they were going to use.

He waited as they rose up on the wheel and could see London all lit up below them. And then he took a deep breath. 'OK. Here's the thing. When I was twenty, I had plans to get married. It didn't work out—for a lot of reasons—and I got married to someone else. So did the girl I originally wanted to marry. It didn't work out for either of us. And I think that's because we married the wrong person—we should've married each other.'

Her face was white.

'Alex,' he said softly. 'We've both made mistakes. And I can understand if you don't ever want to get married again. So I'm not asking you that. I'm just asking you to be with me.'

At the top of the curve, he took the velvet-covered box from his pocket, dropped onto one knee and took her hand. 'Alex, you're the one who completes me. When I'm with you, everything fits and it's in the right place. I love you. And I want to be with you.' He opened the box. 'I'd marry you in a heartbeat, but this isn't an engagement ring to pressure you. It's an eternity ring, and I've spent weeks talking to that designer who did the pop-up shop you organised.'

Alexandra's face cleared. 'So that's why she's been running all those designs past me?'

'Yup. I wanted to give you a surprise—but I wanted it to be something I knew you would choose to wear, not someone else's thoughts of what you ought to wear.'

'Oh, Jordan.' Her eyes filled with tears.

'I've always loved you. I'll love you for the rest of my life. That's what this ring is about. It's not a shackle, it's a promise. Every time you doubt me, you can look at this ring and know that I'll love you for eternity.' He dragged in a breath. 'We don't have to get married and it doesn't matter if we don't have children. What matters to me is being with you. I love you, Alex. And I think you love me. So how about us giving each other a chance to be really happy?'

She nodded. 'Oh. Jordan. The ring's absolutely beautiful.'

She'd said yes. He only realised then that he'd stopped breathing, waiting for her answer. He kissed the fourth finger of her right hand and slipped the ring over the top of his kiss.

'Actually, I do have a question.' She waited for him to look her in the eye. 'Jordan Smith, will you marry me?'

It was the last thing he'd expected. He stared at her in utter disbelief. 'You're asking me to marry you?'

'You have a point. We both had a marriage that didn't work out because we married the wrong person.' She stroked his face. 'You're not Nathan. You'd never try to control me. You'd be bossy, yes, but you'd expect me to be just as bossy back. And I trust you. I know you'd never hurt me, never try to make me be anything other than who I am.'

'Never,' he confirmed softly.

She took the ring off her finger and handed it back to him. 'So are you going to do this thing properly, this time?'

'But—Alex, this isn't an engagement ring.'

'It's beautiful. It's exactly what I would've chosen. And if we're going to finish building those bridges with our parents and have dinner with them to celebrate our engagement, that ring really needs to be on my left hand, don't you think?'

She was really going to do it. She was going to marry

him, and finish building bridges with both their families.
Make their future whole. Jordan's smile was so wide that it
felt as if it reached across the whole of London. 'Alexandra,
I love you. Will you do me the honour of being my wife?'

She smiled back at him. 'I thought you'd never ask. Yes.'

He slipped the ring onto the fourth finger of her left
hand, this time. And he was laughing as he got to his feet,
pulled her into his arms and kissed her.

* * * * *

Mills & Boon® Hardback
March 2012

ROMANCE

Roccanti's Marriage Revenge	Lynne Graham
The Devil and Miss Jones	Kate Walker
Sheikh Without a Heart	Sandra Marton
Savas's Wildcat	Anne McAllister
The Argentinian's Solace	Susan Stephens
A Wicked Persuasion	Catherine George
Girl on a Diamond Pedestal	Maisey Yates
The Theotokis Inheritance	Susanne James
The Good, the Bad and the Wild	Heidi Rice
The Ex Who Hired Her	Kate Hardy
A Bride for the Island Prince	Rebecca Winters
Pregnant with the Prince's Child	Raye Morgan
The Nanny and the Boss's Twins	Barbara McMahon
Once a Cowboy...	Patricia Thayer
Mr Right at the Wrong Time	Nikki Logan
When Chocolate Is Not Enough...	Nina Harrington
Sydney Harbour Hospital: Luca's Bad Girl	Amy Andrews
Falling for the Sheikh She Shouldn't	Fiona McArthur

HISTORICAL

Untamed Rogue, Scandalous Mistress	Bronwyn Scott
Honourable Doctor, Improper Arrangement	Mary Nichols
The Earl Plays With Fire	Isabelle Goddard
His Border Bride	Blythe Gifford

MEDICAL

Dr Cinderella's Midnight Fling	Kate Hardy
Brought Together by Baby	Margaret McDonagh
The Firebrand Who Unlocked His Heart	Anne Fraser
One Month to Become a Mum	Louisa George

Mills & Boon® Large Print

March 2012

ROMANCE

The Power of Vasilii — Penny Jordan
The Real Rio D'Aquila — Sandra Marton
A Shameful Consequence — Carol Marinelli
A Dangerous Infatuation — Chantelle Shaw
How a Cowboy Stole Her Heart — Donna Alward
Tall, Dark, Texas Ranger — Patricia Thayer
The Boy is Back in Town — Nina Harrington
Just An Ordinary Girl? — Jackie Braun

HISTORICAL

The Lady Gambles — Carole Mortimer
Lady Rosabella's Ruse — Ann Lethbridge
The Viscount's Scandalous Return — Anne Ashley
The Viking's Touch — Joanna Fulford

MEDICAL

Cort Mason – Dr Delectable — Carol Marinelli
Survival Guide to Dating Your Boss — Fiona McArthur
Return of the Maverick — Sue MacKay
It Started with a Pregnancy — Scarlet Wilson
Italian Doctor, No Strings Attached — Kate Hardy
Miracle Times Two — Josie Metcalfe

0212 GEN STD LP

Mills & Boon® Hardback

April 2012

ROMANCE

A Deal at the Altar	Lynne Graham
Return of the Moralis Wife	Jacqueline Baird
Gianni's Pride	Kim Lawrence
Undone by his Touch	Annie West
The Legend of de Marco	Abby Green
Stepping out of the Shadows	Robyn Donald
Deserving of his Diamonds?	Melanie Milburne
Girl Behind the Scandalous Reputation	Michelle Conder
Redemption of a Hollywood Starlet	Kimberly Lang
Cracking the Dating Code	Kelly Hunter
The Cattle King's Bride	Margaret Way
Inherited: Expectant Cinderella	Myrna Mackenzie
The Man Who Saw Her Beauty	Michelle Douglas
The Last Real Cowboy	Donna Alward
New York's Finest Rebel	Trish Wylie
The Fiancée Fiasco	Jackie Braun
Sydney Harbour Hospital: Tom's Redemption	Fiona Lowe
Summer With A French Surgeon	Margaret Barker

HISTORICAL

Dangerous Lord, Innocent Governess	Christine Merrill
Captured for the Captain's Pleasure	Ann Lethbridge
Brushed by Scandal	Gail Whitiker
Lord Libertine	Gail Ranstrom

MEDICAL

Georgie's Big Greek Wedding?	Emily Forbes
The Nurse's Not-So-Secret Scandal	Wendy S. Marcus
Dr Right All Along	Joanna Neil
Doctor on Her Doorstep	Annie Claydon

0312 GEN STD HB

Mills & Boon® Large Print

April 2012

ROMANCE

Jewel in His Crown	Lynne Graham
The Man Every Woman Wants	Miranda Lee
Once a Ferrara Wife...	Sarah Morgan
Not Fit for a King?	Jane Porter
Snowbound with Her Hero	Rebecca Winters
Flirting with Italian	Liz Fielding
Firefighter Under the Mistletoe	Melissa McClone
The Tycoon Who Healed Her Heart	.Melissa James

HISTORICAL

The Lady Forfeits	Carole Mortimer
Valiant Soldier, Beautiful Enemy	Diane Gaston
Winning the War Hero's Heart	Mary Nichols
Hostage Bride	Anne Herries

MEDICAL

Breaking Her No-Dates Rule	Emily Forbes
Waking Up With Dr Off-Limits	Amy Andrews
Tempted by Dr Daisy	Caroline Anderson
The Fiancée He Can't Forget	Caroline Anderson
A Cotswold Christmas Bride	Joanna Neil
All She Wants For Christmas	Annie Claydon

0312 GEN STD LP

MR